CASCADE

THE SEVERANCE: BOOK 1

SUZANNE HAGELIN

CASCADE

Kierkad and his brother Sentinels are ready to die for the Noble Call of protecting humanity. They gave up everything, their home world, identity, and memories of the past for the privilege.

One day, the Cascade begins to fall from the skies, a virus guided by sentient thought with dread purpose, and Sentinels begin to disappear. As their numbers decrease, Kierkad's world is fracturing. He is forced to face that nothing is what it seems.

The Noble Call has become a trap.

For Henry

CONTENTS

CHAPTER 1

Three Weeks

With noble goal we walk the streets.
With noble heart we uphold peace.
With noble zeal we combat threats.
All storms of war will cease.
—The Sentinel's Call

Ka-thump. Ka-thump. Ka-thump.

The hollow pounding resonated from the Sentinel's chest up into his head. For just a moment, everything around him was alien and alarming. The colors and smells, the moving figures and sounds, all clashing against him in uneven ripples. Nothing made sense.

Two small beings shuffled up the strip of concrete heading in his direction, delicate, miniature versions of humans. His arm began to rise, and his fingers extended toward them as if to point, the silver white color of his armor shimmered and darkened. Flashes of images and thought jabbed across his consciousness in a confusing swirl. Crayons scratching on yellow paper. Dark metal arms slicing through the air. Wailing voices. Base notes in agitated rhythms. Voices and cries. *Come back. Go away.* Fear. Fury.

Eyes.

I have eyes, he thought, as he scanned around him slowly, reconnecting with the present world and its inhabitants again, pushing against the disorientation and confusion.

Eyes are the link, he added, remembering that he had two means of communication with the beings. Words and eyes. Information was traded with words. Eyes could… he wasn't sure what they did. He gathered visual data, but communication, how was that done and why did he think this way? His eyes *saw*, but no links were made, and the result was pain in his torso.

Deep within, the Indoctriny surged, quieting the chaos in his mind, relieving him of the clashing and thumping. Quiet fell in the chambers of his body, in his mind, in his innermost center. For a moment, anguish hung there in the emptiness, loneliness too deep to face, a wordless sorrow. It sat there in the center, soaking up the noise until it had ended, then it sunk within him. Deeper than awareness, deeper than feeling, deeper than the state of being he recognized as life.

In its place, happiness stirred, and his arm lowered back to his side. As the Indoctriny restored him, he forgot that he had felt anything at all. He remembered his name and readdressed his present assignment with joy.

Kierkad continued down the sidewalk at a steady, smooth tempo, a musical meter suitable for Sousa. His joints were warm, his limbs fluid, his movements effortless. He turned his head to one side and then the other, surveying his route with pride.

The two children walked toward him, their hair blowing gently as they moved, their clothes swishing, their shoes making soft whispery noises.

He smiled at them. *I am your peace*, he thought, as he nodded slightly. *Be at ease.*

The smaller one, a younger sister perhaps, lifted her eyes to his face, and smiled faintly. But the other one had noticed the uplifted arm Kierkad had now forgotten.

Kierkad paused and leaned toward them. His presence instilled comfort, he knew this, yet the older one looked afraid. Her eyes widened, her pupils constricted, her face taut. "You are safe," he reassured her. "I am here and there is nothing to fear." His words only distressed her more. She yanked on her younger sister's hand and pulled her sideways around him, moving quickly in little sidesteps. It pierced him with concern.

"I am good," he said, his voice conveying none of the anxiety her look caused. "I will take care of your neighborhood and all of you. My life is devoted to this, and I will not fail you."

They fled. He turned and watched them over his shoulder as they ran.

It hadn't always been this way. When he had first been assigned to the Valley of Gentle Hearts, the people had followed his regular patrols with glistening eyes full of hope, waving, even blowing him kisses. Children had come to him with flowers and cards.

Adults had stopped to thank him and shake his hand. He had been one of the deliverers.

Now, they feared him. It wasn't right. *I have been your hope*, he thought, wondering if his eyes were able to portray hurt feelings. Was his armor human enough? Was his face expressive through the transparent mask? He didn't know. There were no mirrors at the Harbor and when he looked in them at other places, he didn't know how to interpret what he saw. A man shaped figure with man eyes and man movements. It meant nothing.

"We are glad you're here, Sentinel," a woman with a leather bag over her shoulder paused near him. "The children don't understand. They never saw what it was like before. Now, with the Cascade and all, they're just frightened by whatever seems... out of place." She nodded and walked away not waiting for a reply.

He watched her. An instantaneous scan brought up her identity and history, more about her than she knew herself, but none of it mattered in his foremost thoughts. He could only allow certain facts to rest there. This legal office person was a distraction.

Her words, though, were helpful. I should not mind the children's fear or need the woman's explanation, he reprimanded himself. I am selfless and noble. I am here for their good, even if they don't understand. I love them and will always love them. This is who I am.

A soul full of purpose kept him mentally ready for the next assault. The body wasn't a problem. He could always count on the strength and drive he needed to battle any enemy and overcome any obstacle. The Harbor existed to keep him and his comrades in perfect working order.

Kierkad began his march again, humming inside his mask at a pitch only he could hear, walking in the steady pace that fit the music, smiling as he scanned the streets, sidewalks, yards, parks, and houses on his path. He would guard his people and if he died in the process, another noble one like himself would take his place.

The Harbor, the massive compound that housed the Sentinels, was firmly planted in a vast space along the Brave River, glowing with light, like a beacon of promise. Kierkad's heart swelled with pride and joy as he spied it in the distance. It was his home and refuge—not that he needed one so elaborate, but it was given to him all the same.

He had no memory of the life he had lived before. When he had given up his former self to become a Sentinel, he had given up *everything* and only a clean wipe made that possible. The rumors about his background rolled around the valley as people wondered what planet he came from, what species he was, what his native language had been, what his real features were like. These rumors captivated him as much as they did the people. He toyed with them and laughed at them. He shared the most outlandish ones with his brothers. They were in it together. It was good.

The alarms equipped in his face-shield began wailing, starting with a deep, low-decibel base note and rising quickly in pitch to a pure-toned high note that broke into staccato dashes. As soon as the note struck twelve times, the base note began again, almost inaudibly.

The Cascade.

Kirkad ran. He carried emergency gear, but it was better if he could get to his pod and search from there. Within three alarms he had reached where it was parked at the end of the street and dived in, in one seamless motion, turning as he arced to fall into the scooped chair molded for his body. The door sealed behind him and the pod throbbed as he powered up. His mind vaulted into the skies as a winged sensor took off from the top of the pod, a meter-long, ultra-thin boomerang shaped drone—his avatar, his alter-ego, his flying self.

Up into the clouds he soared, no longer aware of the clunky earth form deposited in the pod. *Frrrrrinnnngggg!* His bladed wings vibrated in a metallic hum as he sped upward. Seconds counted. The faster the response, the better the chance that the Cascade would be countered in time, and lives would be spared. Not civilian lives, there had never actually been any deaths among the helpless citizenry. The Sentinels were good at what they did and had a perfect record of protection, even from the first days of the invasion.

The loss of Sentinels was the key danger. And the more that perished, the higher the chance that one day the Cascade would break through their defenses and decimate the peaceful population. Or an invading force returned from the old adversary.

The earth was a checkerboard of fields and neighborhoods now as he blasted his way higher and higher into the stratosphere. Still no visible floats.

The humming of other Sentinels aloft in their avatars began to fill his ears. Many of his brothers were being added to the fight, building a crescendo of counterforce, striving against gravity to reach the enemy who merely had to fall to reach the target.

There! Light glanced off one like a sparkle of sunlight on lapping water. Then another… and another. Soon the sparkles were flickering all around

Kierkad and his brothers on every side. It was a massive fall with thousands of flimsy, jellyfish-bodied traps wafting down.

They were easy to destroy. That wasn't the problem. But there were so many of them and not one could be allowed to touch the ground. The winged avatars screamed through the skies, back and forth, all over, slashing them into shreds with a mere passing through them, slicing them with the edge of the wings. The chip they carried would never make it to the surface intact.

Sunlight gleamed golden on the Sentinel drones like flame, brilliant and beautiful against the semi-darkened blue sky, like flashes of gilded lightning painted in broad strokes on the background of floating sparks.

Kierkad kept count. Twenty. Forty. Sixty. It was easier to flame through many in the beginning. When they grew sparse, it was harder to catch or even see them, and the numbers he destroyed added up more slowly.

On the ground, he could still experience motion. He felt his pod shake and thud as he jumped, jolted, jerked to the right or the left, unable to separate the movement of the drone from the action of his body. He was sweating and his heart was pounding in his chest.

"Auugghhh!" he yelled involuntarily as his winged drone sliced into that of another brother, like swords clashing, hooking, and sliding to the hilts in a fencing match. Metallic rings and crunches blasted through his skull for several split seconds then they flung themselves free and Kierkad whipped away, spinning and falling, falling, falling. The earth enlarged and raced to slam into him as he moaned, dazed and blinking. "No!" he exhorted himself, pulling up on the controls, willing the craft to accelerate out of the dive.

The wings vibrated and strobed him with loud shrieks as he fought to regain control. He could see nothing anymore but stabs of light and dark, shaking violently until an explosion rent his ears. Not the full impact of noise, the pod dulled it enough to spare his hearing, but enough to give him understanding of the craft's demise. It had autodestructed to avoid causing damage on impact.

He opened his eyes as the pod door swung out, noticing as he always did that climbing out was nothing like jumping in. His body was trembling, and his legs were unsteady. His vision blurred as he blinked repeatedly. Around the pod, bystanders stood in scattered groups watching him. He was unable to read their expressions. That part of his brain function would return when he had had time to recoup at the base.

Once his feet were placed on the ground, he leaned onto the roof of the pod and took deep breaths to steady himself. His audio was giving him updates as he waited.

"…seventeen more floats flamed… two brothers out of play… twenty-three floats destroyed… searching… searching… three floats identified… two more floats detected… searching… searching… none detected… confirmed: all eliminated…"

The voice never announced how many brothers were lost till later, in the safety of the Harbor.

"The danger is over," Kierkad turned and informed the bystanders. Some sighed in visible relief. Others merely nodded and turned to go. A few children were scattered among them, clinging to the hands of adults or friends, staring at him with large eyes. He wondered if they were associating him with the danger instead of the protection. The look in their eyes was confusing and he never remembered to ask what it meant once he was restored to full function.

The patrol he had begun would be finished by a fresh Sentinel. His strength was spent, and he had to get back to base before he collapsed. Losing an avatar was particularly weakening and the feeling of helplessness at having no means to fight brought with it a heavy sense of dread.

Kierkad climbed back into the pod and hit the auto-sequence for home, then closed his eyes, clinging fiercely to the armrests, and compelled himself to remain calm till he could be re-stabilized. He felt sick. Down to his bones.

In the Harbor, the pod slotted into park and he was lifted out by the robotic restorators. He had watched them retrieve other brothers and knew that sometimes they moaned or even made sounds like weeping. Some thrashed and fought the care as though they had forgotten it was vital to their health. He was unaware of any noise or movement on his own part and wondered distractedly if he were resisting in some way. His mind seemed to have withdrawn from the surroundings; they were foggy and muffled, far away, dreamlike.

On one side, he saw and heard the activity of the restorators, snapping him into the gurney, carting him along, attaching tubes, clicking buttons on his face-shield. On the other, darkness—quiet, warm, safe— beckoned and wooed him. He turned toward it and let it envelope him.

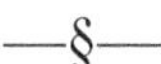

"Rise up, Noble Sentinel," the restorator greeted him.

Kierkad's heart swelled with pride as he swung his legs over the side of the cot and sat up. *I am noble,* he remembered with a surge of joy in his chest, *I have battled and survived. Once again, I rise up to defend those I love.*

"I am well," he responded, turning to gaze at the robot that stared at him with a mild, featureless face.

Stretching out an arm, he extended and flexed his fingers, rotating the hand as he tested them. They worked flawlessly, joints fluid, tendons strong, muscles elastic. On the inside of his wrist, the emblem of the Sentinel, etched in black, rippled gently with the motion of his fingers.

Sometimes, he would stare at it. Alone at night in his bunk, he would pull up his sleeve and stare at the place where he knew it to be, as though communing with it, melding his mind with it. And he would imagine that it glowed in a deep, blueish hue, humming. He would hum with it, not aloud, but in his mind. *There,* he would think to himself. *There I am.*

But now, in full light of day, this seemed childish and distant. He clapped his hands onto the cot on either side of him and with a light push, jumped to his feet, standing.

"Kierkad, Sentinel Kan-B-49-L-16, reporting," he announced, "Ready for duty." He pulled himself upright, tightening with a snap, an immovable pillar of solidity, arms at his side, feet together, eyes forward.

"You are released," the restorator replied.

Breaking into a trot, Kierkad sped out the door.

—§—

A roar of voices greeted him as he entered the mess. Clashing sounds echoed as he slammed his forearm against a brother's forearm, then another and another, a loud cacophony of cheerfulness, anchoring the assurance of belonging—of home. This was his place. He was a hero. They were all there to be noble, and it was good.

"What?" Sedakad hollered at him, slamming both forearms against his, then banging him with his head and grabbing his shoulders with both hands. "Cutting me out of the sky?"

"Was it you?" Kierkad laughed and punched his stomach with both fists. They roared and threw a few more punches.

"You anarchist!" his brother stepped away, leaning backward slightly, as if overcome with laughter, without the sound of it. "You're going to get a bad name if you keep that up!"

"Me?" Kierkad leaned over resting his hands on his knees, acting tired, which he wasn't, watching for the next move. "You knocked me out of the sky, and I had to autodestruct. I'll be out of commission till I get a new drone. You're the anarchist!"

"You slammed me—and I autodestructed long before you did, Kier," he lunged and Kierkad caught him in a hug as they toppled over, yelling, rolling around.

"Sentinels," the somber voice emanated through the hall. The lights dimmed and brightened three times, and all the brothers rose to attention.

Kierkad and Sedakad jumped to their feet, pulling each other up, and stood side by side.

Pacificator Nirekad, robed to his feet in black trimmed in deep blue, strode into the hall with a calm humility that belied the palpable air of authority. More than respected, he was loved and feared by the brothers.

"Well done, Sentinels," he said, his words stirring pride in every listening heart. "You have won the battle. Every float of the Cascade was destroyed before touching the ground."

He paused. The emotion the news caused rolled around them as if they had applauded, though they made no sound.

"Two brothers collided mid-air," a murmured groan was heard on many sides. "You should all be commended for your flying. These instances are very rare and can happen to anyone. Let no one curse the brothers who were thus cut down, mid-battle, and unable to finish. The disappointment is rebuke enough."

He turned and let his gaze fall on the two brothers. Kierkad trembled inside and was glad his eyes were tearless. Grief over the disappointment flooded him.

"These are noble brothers who have done well," the Pacificator continued and Kierkad's heart soared at the reprieve. "Tomorrow," he added, turning away to look around at the others, "it may be one of you. And we will not shame you for something you did not seek out."

The entire hall grew lighter.

"Some of you are missing..." Pacificator Nirekad raised his voice. Many of the brothers hung their heads. Some folded their arms across their chests and stared off to the side. A few mumbled. Kierkad's heart sunk as he waited for the rest of the report.

"Brothers Uyalkad, Traekad, Perakad, Chordkad, Malikad, Gankad..."

"No!" One of the listeners called out. "Not Gankad! My brother!"

"Erdakad, Weirkad..." Several more voices complained.

The list went on. Twenty-three brothers were MIA.

Experience had proven that they would never be retrieved.

"As you know well," the Pacificator concluded, "These brothers have given their lives for a noble cause... as have you. They are missed but their memories are exalted. We have not yet obtained their bodies, and therefore we hope—we continue to hope, that some may yet be found alive."

He paused as the barely tangible hope sunk into their understanding and faded away without finding roots.

"We have an even greater hope that we will decipher the Cascade's methods and counter them. We will learn to anticipate their attacks. We will one day launch an assault on *their* bases and wipe them out at the source. We will eliminate this threat once and for all. Never again will our planet be threatened by invasion."

He stood at the center of the hall, turning slowly on his feet as he spoke, touching each one with his gaze, pulling them together, strengthening their hope and resolve.

"We have an even greater hope than this," he said. "We will uphold the noble realm for all humans. We will live nobly and with honor. We will grant our beloved flock, our human children, our treasure, a home that is safe, without danger or suffering or hardship, and they will never again shed a tear, and their children will not know the meaning of the word 'fear'..."

The brothers were moved. Each one had given themselves freely to this vision. They loved the humans in their care, their flock.

"You are noble," he said.

"We are noble," they thundered in one voice.

"You are guardians of the realm," he said.

"We are Sentinels," they boomed as one.

"You are not loved but you love."

"We love the people."

"You will live for them."

"And we will die for them!"

"You are noble."

"We are noble! We live for the noble realm!"

Silence in the wake of these shouts felt like noise of an opposite quality. Pacificator Nirekad turned and walked out of the hall. Behind, the brothers relaxed and went back to their meal.

Kierkad and Sedakad sat next to one another. Food was placed before them by the mess hall droid. It was bland and satisfying. Food was never anything else.

"I don't understand," Sedakad murmured between bites.

Kierkad glanced at him sideways. They weren't kept from speaking about these things, but it was discouraged in an unspoken way, the way all their behavior was guided, through unseen pushes, motivating, resisting, accepting, deterring. Kier knew that for Sedakad to speak those words, he had to lean against the compulsion he felt to not say them.

"How does the Cascade..." he fell silent. He must've been daunted by the resistance.

Kierkad looked back down at his food. He wondered, too. How did the Cascade decide when and where to attack? What was it? What was the point?

CASCADE

Why did they look so harmless and yet cause so much damage?

There were many questions.

Sedakad clenched his jaw for a moment. "Why..." he growled through gritted teeth, "do they..." Long, awkward pauses punctuated the rest. "...go after... us? ...and... what happens to... the brothers... they... they... they..." He began choking.

Someone grabbed him from behind and with a thrust of his fist against his chest, popped a piece of food out of his throat. He gasped and spat it out onto his plate. Looking over at Kierkad, he squinted in anger, glared at him.

"You're alright," someone said.

Sedakad shook his head vehemently, but what came out was, "Yes." Then he walked away.

Kierkad didn't watch him leave but he felt a twinge of secret guilt toward him. Guilt was not encouraged. More than that, it didn't seem to exist among them, though the word was known. It was used in training sessions to help them understand the people they protected. It was never included in their home at the Harbor.

But he felt it and covered it up. Seda had tried to talk to him. For a moment they had been closer to each other than to the other brothers, sharing the mishap. The momentary reproof had given them something unique in common. And at that moment, Seda had reached out with a burden he was tired of carrying. Kier carried it too. They all did. What did it matter if they talked about it to each other?

Somehow, the code of the Sentinels kept them silent. They couldn't speak of their concerns or doubts. Their questions had to be kept in, waiting for answers, perhaps never to be answered.

Sedakad had struggled to voice one, reaching out for help, and Kierkad had let him flounder and offered him nothing.

If you ignore the hand stretched out to you, the code said, one day you will reach out and be ignored.

Suppression had kept him from responding but he might one day regret it.

CASCADE

CHAPTER 2

18 Days

*"As servants of humankind, we lay down our thoughts,
our hours, our minds for this one great calling:
to build a noble future for those who are higher than us.
We have no need for a name or a memory."*
—The Order, *"Pensées of Indoctriny"*, stanzas 37-38

Bonding was a weekly requirement. There were seventy-eight sentinels stationed at the Harbor and they were always kept to a full complement, with new brothers being added within hours to replace those lost in battle. Harmonizing minds and syncing bio-vibrations required regular training.

I hate this, Kierkad found the thread of a thought nagging in the back of his mind, behind the visible places open to the Harbor. It had shown up before, but he never remembered it till it popped up again. The weight of Indoctriny compelled him to march to the resonance hall and he obeyed without question. But in his bowels, or whatever the lower regions of his torso should be called—that was another thought that came up sometimes and was forgotten afterward—a deep aversion resisted.

He quelled it as he always did.

Sentinels lined up in six rows of thirteen, three sets facing each other, standing an arm's length apart. Silence filled the hall as they locked gazes and stared at one another. Face to face. Eyes to eyes. Mind to mind.

Rage to rage.

It always started with rage, as if the two brothers were wild beasts forced into a cage together, bodies rigid, claws bound, jaws clenched, unable to snarl—restricted inside an unmoving body with only the window of the eyes to express the fury.

Kierkad, body locked in a position of attention, faced a new brother. He had bulging brown eyes with sparks of yellow. The eyelids were rimmed with red. The brows trembled with anger. As he stared at him, Kier found himself astonished at the hatred he saw there. His heart caved inside of him as though he were afraid.

But he knew that only anger would be expressed in his own face. And he felt that also. His own eyes bulging, his eyebrows quivering, the blood rushing to his forehead. The brother would never see the fear.

"Sentinels," Nirekad, their master, spoke. "Meeting. Forward."

Without hesitation, every sentinel in the room took a step forward and found themselves pressed body to body, face to face, mask to mask right at the tip of their noses. Magnets pulled them against each other, and they began to grit their teeth and curl their lips. The rage rose in a crescendo as they were unable to separate or even close their eyes.

Enforced intimacy, wordless and comfortless, gripped them in a vise. If they had been free to move, they would've fought to the death. If they could've spoken, their words would have been guttural cries of pain.

"You are filled with anger," Nirekad said.

The brothers, pressed in pairs in rows of thirteen, wrestled within the confines of their armored bodies and the racket filled the room like the crashing of heavy machinery.

"Why?" The master asked.

The crashing began to find a rhythm, harmonizing from random noises to synchronous thrashes.

"Why do you hate your brother?"

The noise oscillated in a sine wave, flanging thin and broad. Kier found himself moaning inside but no sound escaped his lips. He was a part of the noise without making any. He always forgot about this later.

"Why do you hate me?" Nirekad's voice no longer seemed outside of him. He was thinking these words.

"I hate you," said the master, but his words were echoing in their minds. Every brother thought these words together. *I hate you. I hate you. I hate you.* It throbbed in their heads till a new anguish broke out and the master spoke the very words they were just beginning to utter in their souls.

"I am alone." A distress far greater than the rage overflowed from inside them, racking their bodies with pain, and the hate dissipated like smoke. The mechanical crashes in the room died down. A new sound built up in the resonance hall and rumbled through them.

It was sorrowful and majestic.

"I am with you." The words of the master burst into their consciousness and once again they noticed the eyes of the brother they each faced. Pain, sorrow, and loneliness flickered there, and from that a new understanding sparked.

The sounds grew in pitch and resolved into something melodic.

"I am your brother." Understanding broadened into bonding. Sharing the pain numbed the sorrow and quenched the loneliness, and in the hall the music mounted with grandeur.

Kier stared at the brother he had hated, the brother he had been hated by, the one he loved, and wished he could weep. The eyes before him echoed a similar longing. It pulled their hearts toward each other, two souls clutching at warmth, at meaning. He grasped at Kier desperately with those eyes and Kier responded in like anguish. A wordless cry burst from his throat.

"I love you." Words from the master's lips spoke for them.

The music slammed in a clamorous chord full of triumph, a completion that broke their containment and released them from its bonds.

The brothers wrapped their arms around their partners with shouts of joy and embraced as one. United. Harmonious.

Restored.

—§—

The Valley of Gentle Hearts hadn't always been known by that name. The devastation the former town had suffered at the hands of the enemy had been so severe that the survivors had begged for a new one. History books were useless now, filled with accounts of unknown cities and regions no one could find. Their heritage had become meaningless. They just couldn't reach out and identify with it anymore.

All around them, gardens grew and flourished with flowers and trees, crops and abundance. The river flowed with fresh water, and the seasons and the weather cycled as they always had. They had homes, jobs, community, and purpose. Tales of famine and disease, war and mass destruction, fear and despair—all this was foreign to them, and many considered it a lie.

"There never was such a thing," were murmurs that were heard when they were mentioned.

"Hush!" others would caution. "Only because of our guardians. Don't let them hear you!"

But they did hear. The Sentinels could hear better than the people realized, and these doubts and whispers were reassuring to them. They were the normal mumblings of a healthy society where skepticism and pride could flourish as much as good will and common sense.

The Severing had nearly wiped out the human race. No one doubted that. Everyone knew that if the Sentinels hadn't appeared to rescue them, the extinction would have been complete. But they *had* come, glistening spaceships in the sky, glowing with rainbow-edged white light, their vessels screaming through the skies in deafening banshee shrieks, landing and disemboweling waves upon waves of peacekeepers that spread out like locusts, consuming everything in their path.

The enemy had fallen before the unrelenting advance. Black armored alien creatures with multiple limbs equipped with blades, guns, and other weapons had been trampled underfoot, squashed, and vanquished.

The victors had walked every inch of the captive terrain and when it was liberated, stood on hilltops around the realm, brightly lit beacons in human form—smiling.

"We love you and we are here to bring you peace and safety," they had announced in thundering unison, soundwaves that spread around the planet.

"At last! At last!" the survivors had cried over and over, weeping, cheering, crawling out of holes and broken doors, ragged in the remnants of their clothing.

There were so many recordings of that day that no one would ever doubt it had taken place, no matter how many years went by, no matter how many generations were to come. Those who had survived and lived to see the recovery still walked among the people. Their stories remained vivid, and they were regarded with respect.

When that generation passed and newer ones took their place who had nothing but recordings and books to teach them, the Sentinels would still be there, living testimonies to the greatest rescue ever accomplished in human history.

—§—

Kierkad couldn't recall the great battles at all, though he knew he had been a part of the invasion force. His injuries must have been too serious. He did remember working on the land, rebuilding homes, laying out and planting gardens, reassuring people day after day that they were there to keep them safe… that they wouldn't leave them to the mercy of the Severance again. The bad aliens would never regain power.

The shadow of the dark oppressor still lurked in the recesses of people's minds, but no one asked who they were, or where they had come from, or why they had come and caused so much anguish. Even Kier wondered sometimes though he wasn't supposed to. One of the brothers had asked about them in the early days and the answer was engraved on his mind.

"You will never ask about this again. To remain in the peace which is your heritage and retain your joy in the guardianship entrusted to you, you must never think of it again. It is not for you to know. Even I must forget what I know." The highest leader under Vil Darad, QruDarad, the Conciliator, had been the one speaking these words.

Kier must have seen the aliens, but he only remembered a child's picture, drawn in their recovery period when such things were allowed because they were helpful for mental healing. He had kept it. He had folded the paper and put it in a crack in the wall behind his bunk. It might not be there any longer. Cleanser drones may have swept it away in a weekly cycle, but he never checked. He wanted to believe it was still there. And he could bring it to mind whenever he wished.

It showed a black, misshapen thing, like a crooked spider with squiggly antenna on top standing on two curved legs, and ghastly limbs pointing in several directions. Three people in the picture ran from it screaming. One smaller one, presumably the child who drew the picture, cried and held onto something like a cat, staring at the alien. One limb, jagged like the teeth of a saw, hung over its head.

Unharmed, he reminded himself. He didn't know if he was the Sentinel who rescued the child before it was killed, but he liked to think so. The child had lived to tell the tale in crayon.

He was lying in the dark in the middle of the night, flat on his back with his arms crossed over his chest. The emblem of the Sentinels was pressed against where his heart would be—if he were human, if he had one. He didn't know. That was a topic the Indoctriny prevented him from pondering. His teeth clenched and he shuddered as he rushed to find other ideas to distract him. Sleep had been more problematic since the crash of his drone but for some reason he liked being wakeful in the night. It was stolen, secret.

Perhaps Seda was awake as well.

He sat up. There was no harm in finding out, was there? No inner pressure restrained him, so he rose to his feet tossing aside the metallic cover and left the room.

The hallways were made of stone with concrete floors and lit by long bands of yellow light along the floor and ceiling. He looked both ways, untouched by emotion of any kind. The bare walls and dim lighting were neither soothing nor forlorn. They were functional. Kier turned to the left, walked to the end of the hall and climbed a ladder to the next level up. Several doors down he reached Seda's door and knocked.

Thud. Thud. Thud. He wondered if he had always knocked in threes. It seemed appropriate… routine.

Without waiting for an answer, he opened the door and went in to see his brother sitting upright, staring at him.

"I am Kier," he said, assuming the dim lights would make it hard to see.

Seda stared.

Kier stared back.

Transparent masks were worn over their heads, even at night, but this wasn't what hid the faces within. There was a deeper mask, layered over their minds by the indoctrination, that veiled them even when they could see each other clearly. They had never looked at each other and seen what eyes were meant to see in another face—a person.

Kier saw a soul looking back at him. Someone who was troubled, puzzled, who searched his face and wondered. Seda gazed at him as if he were…human.

It was unnerving.

Kier stiffened with instinctual alarm and the look in Seda's eyes grew frightened, then desperate. He glanced around rapidly, scanning for danger, and brought his eyes back to Kier, focusing on him with an air of warning, as if to say, back away!

Kier backed away, out of the room, closing the door behind him. Trembling, he returned to his bunk and lay back down. The peace techniques he normally used to calm himself would work well, but he hesitated. Once he began them, he wouldn't care anymore. He wouldn't try to understand or even to remember the strange interchange. He would forget the *person* he saw, the thoughts and emotions that flickered there. The link to someone under the mask would be shattered.

Pain ached in his heart, and he felt…lonely.

It grew stronger until it triggered a response and his training kicked in, taking over, subduing and extinguishing the longing he felt. With a deep sigh, he fell asleep and didn't move till morning.

The next Cascade fell a number of miles away and Sentinels from several bases responded. Kier raced in his pod across the valley and up the long slope of the mountains, heading for the pass, heedless of the snow and ice on the roads. The pod sped better on its air cushion over cold surfaces.

He was anxious to try his new avatar drone. There had been a number of upgrades installed because of the previous attack, capitalizing on weaknesses discovered in the enemy's tactics, whatever those were. There were some new collision-avoidance tactics as well, magnetic repelling and preprogrammed responses. He looked forward to trying them out.

"Largest fall in weeks," the audio informed. "Twelve units are being dispatched. High risk of collision."

The Sentinels were in full battle before Kier and his brothers crested the mountain pass and began the steep descent to the region in danger. It would be fifteen minutes at least before they could engage drones and join the fight. The whirring and humming, yells and updates, filled their ears.

Soon they could see the glimmering lights ahead, filling the sky like stars. No matter how many were eliminated though, there were more to take their place. It seemed unending.

It was standard procedure for the Sentinels to fan out in their pods before stopping and taking off. This was in case a float made it through the net and hit the ground. They could withdraw from the avatar, letting it land on autopilot, and chase down the float in person.

As far as he knew, no one had done this before—but there was always a first time.

Kier deposited his pod on a dirt alley in a small town, hardly more than a hundred homes in size. He was shifting into action inside, preparing for takeoff. *Glide to a stop, park. Lights down. Power up the drone.* It made a low, metallic hum as it geared up for its virgin flight.

Kier paused for a moment to taste the joy of a new drone, just an instant. He smiled and glanced down the alley toward the main road.

Then he saw something.

It didn't make sense.

A figure running. Shaped like a human…with a Sentinel's armor. No, not quite. Darker. Extra limbs.

Kier fumbled and coughed. He stared at the street and the constant updates in his ears from the brothers fighting overhead went unheeded. One second. Two…three seconds.

He coasted the pod down the road a ways, till he could see around the corner—till he could see the shape. There it was. Dark gray, hunched, scuttling along like a bug. It paused at a doorway and, with a punch from a clublike limb, knocked it down.

Sounds from outside the pod were muted but a panel showed a brief loud noise, as if someone had screamed.

Sentinels will protect you. Kierkad was unable to make himself exit the pod. The pressure to engage in the battle overhead was so strong he was helpless to get out and rescue the people in that house. Something like panic mounted within him as he fought to move his hand and open the door to the pod, or even just to broadcast a warning siren.

Inside of himself, other thoughts were rebuking him. Mocking him. Calling him a fool. Telling him to wake up and join his brothers in the *real* fight. The audio of the battle grew louder, and he sunk within himself, pulled toward the avatar, pulled into the winged metal creature that took off with a blaze of burning zeal and exultant joy, whirring up into the skies to the sounds of crashing and the hums of his brothers.

The house, the alley, and the shape all faded.

Glorious in the skies was the flaming of the avatars as they tore through the Cascade, slashing, burning, devastating the falling floats like showers of sparks or fireworks. Kier found himself laughing and the laughter boomed within his chest. Power throbbed in his wings. He dove, dipped, curved, and climbed, swooping around and over, catching one after another after another. The counters rolled without stopping and the brothers cheered. It was intoxicating.

Finally, it ended. Not one had made it to the ground. The drones coasted back to their pods and their awareness distilled back into their bodies.

Kier opened his eyes and looked once again at the street. He saw the house with the busted door, but he hardly knew why it mattered and left it to the local Sentinels to solve.

CHAPTER 3

17 Days

"You are not defined by ancestry or geography. Your identity isn't based on DNA or circuitry. Who you are isn't shaped and taught in schools or homes. You have been dreamed, designed, poured onto visuals, crafted and orchestrated—birthed into being through masterful ingenuity by the Order of the Peace Sentinels. You aren't artificial, but you aren't natural beings either. You're neither humans nor aliens. You must be more than any of these…"
—from Master Sentinel Vil-Darad's commencement speech for the Class of '29

Kier sought out Seda to spar with. He had no clear purpose in mind. It wasn't like he wished to follow up on the strange encounter of the night a few days before.

He just made sure he was near him and they would be paired up for the exercises.

The ritual form was lengthy and entirely memorized. Every step they took, and every blow extended was practiced, always in the same order, with the same impetus, and the same results. If it were less deadly, it would be a form of dance. The shouts and grunts were learned as well, timed for breathing, for resisting, for countering.

If a Sentinel went into hand-to-hand combat and began one of these routines, only another Sentinel would be able to keep up and survive. Anyone else, no matter how powerful or clever, would eventually succumb to the onslaught.

The first round was a five-minute bout with every pair finishing within three seconds of each other. The second was much longer, with repeating segments in patterns, that lasted well over twenty-four minutes, an exhausting drill. More followed of varying length and degrees of difficulty.

Sometimes, at the end of a long day of drills, there would be a moment of comradery, a hint of closeness from the shared experience, a smile, a joke. Kier realized he had been looking for that moment.

"Why…" he ventured in a low voice as they ended the final bout. "Did you… say nothing?" It wasn't suppression that hindered him. He was searching for the right thing to say.

Seda squinted at him sideways. "Why did you?"

Kier was startled by those words. Seda was referring to the other day when he had tried to talk and Kier had said nothing. Why did it surprise him that he would link the two events? Were they linked? Was there a connection? He hadn't expected one—

apparently, he should have—and he felt a deep shock at the lack of continuity inside of himself.

"I have no answer," he replied.

"Neither do I."

Again, there was a flow to these words that Kier struggled to follow. Seda was gauging his behavior by what Kier had done before. How did that work? It was very troubling.

"You don't know…" Seda added, looking at him directly. Kier couldn't see a person behind the mask in daylight, but the idea of a *person* caught him, as if there were *someone* inside who was trying to see him—to see Kier.

Kier stared back at Seda. "Do you?"

Seda searched him with guarded, cautious eyes. "You were awake, and you came looking for me. Why?"

"I've woken up more in the night since our collision. Hours which have been pleasant to me. I thought you might be awake as well and I came to see. To ask…"

"Ask what?"

"What you were thinking about."

"Thinking…" Seda's mouth was partly open with this word, and it hung there as if suspended.

Kier felt the suppression engage inside of him at the same instant Seda began to turn pale and he knew that they both had become the focus of whatever systems were set up to keep them in…keep them in…prime working condition. Of course. Talking about thinking was foolish. Talk is intended for action and communication of important information. That was all that mattered.

He backed away from Seda, whose lips were turning blue, like he was holding his breath.

Kier stopped himself before turning away. That wasn't right. The resistance hindered him, but he found he had the strength to fight it. *I am noble*, he reminded himself. This brother might be in danger. He pushed against the suppression and raised his arms, grasping Seda's shoulders.

"Can you breathe, Brother?" he demanded, shaking him. He searched his databanks for the correct procedure in these cases. Thumping Seda on the back, he sent a distress call to the restoration units.

Seda slumped in his arms but as he was falling, a bare whisper hissed from his lips, a few words only. Having spoken them, he gasped and thrashed and pumped his lungs in a panic, as if he had been bound by them and only set free when they escaped his tongue.

...of being lost... was the phrase that slipped past the constraints of the Indoctriny.

Kier lifted him and carried him down the passageways and was met halfway by the restorators who took Seda and sped away.

Kier stood still and gazed after them long after they were gone.

No one ever thought about being lost. Never. Other brothers were lost. Not us.

Not me.

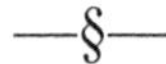

Snow had fallen during the night, blanketing the valley in white. Kier was out on the streets pacing his patrol before the light of day had dawned, cloudy but still bright. The cold was no trouble to him, and he found the air refreshing. The quiet was appealing, too; the sounds of his footsteps barely ruffled it.

He walked, paused, and walked again, circling and combing through his community as the day progressed from morning to afternoon. Nothing sunk into his mind. Snatches of conversation glanced over him and were forgotten.

"I told her to just calm down. It will get better. She needs to stay inside, tend to her daily life, and let things resolve themselves." A reassuring voice drifted out the eaves of the house on the left as Kier moved past.

It pleased him when he heard the flock speaking good words to one another. Peace was a joyful venture and sharing it completed the cycle, making life harmonious in the Valley.

Everything will resolve itself quickly, he thought with a smile. He had heard these sentiments before.

Some children were making a snow fort on the right, accumulating piles of snowballs. Next to them, a neighbor was shoveling snow from his path. Farther down, neighbors were putting seed out for birds, walking dogs, playing with children. On every side there was rest. All was resolved.

What remained unresolved? he wondered abruptly. Why had the voice advised someone to stay calm and stay inside? What did they mean?

He came to a standstill and the people around him stopped what they were doing as well. They turned to look at him, watching him for… for what? Why did they watch him all the time? He rotated slowly, smoothly, catching a glimpse of each expression—frozen into whatever had been there when he stopped.

I don't know, he realized. He couldn't read their faces. He didn't know what they were thinking. He couldn't understand what his part was in their daily lives.

He had never known that he wasn't in harmony with them before.

"I am your friend," he called out. Many nodded. Some called out affirmations, waving and smiling.

The neighbor who had been shoveling came to him with arms outstretched. "We know you are, Sentinel," he said. "Thank you for taking care of us and watching over us."

Kier stared at him unable to clarify his confusion. He held out a hand and the man shook it. "Yes," he said mechanically, looking for words that would solve the confusion.

The man smiled and stepped away, as though not wanting to be rude, but needing to get back to his work.

"Are you happy?" Kier queried. It was directed at the man with the shovel, but he turned to look at others who had approached to include them as well.

"Oh, yes! Of course, we're happy!" they burst out in a chorus with grins and some laughter. "How could we not be? Look at how wonderful our lives are!"

Kier glanced from one to another. *They are happy*, he told himself. *All is well.*

"Are there any problems you need help with?" He extended both hands out. "Are there any issues that need to be resolved?"

"Everything is taken care of," they promised. "We know that you will be here for us if anything comes up."

He nodded and began his patrol again.

A strange splitting sensation took place within him, unlike anything he had ever felt before—a rending, between what he thought underneath and what he allowed his mind to think consciously. He noticed the tearing, without distress, and was amazed at it. He saw two pieces within himself. Two realms. Two levels. He was a divided being. One content with the world and the community around him.

The other…awake and wary.

The Cascade fell again that night and his own treasured Valley was the epicenter. Kier, raised from a dead sleep by the alarms, leapt from the bed and slammed himself into the armor that hung on the wall ready to be clamped on. Joining the mad dash to the pods with his brothers, booted feet pounding the floor in rumbling cacophony, he dove into his seat and sped out of the Harbor docking bay, headed for his assigned station in town.

He was troubled. There was no elation as he burst into the avatar from his pod with more urgency than he had ever known before. Agitation over the threat to his flock was stronger than the excitement that accompanied flying into the high regions of the sky. His underlying self, the one that had torn away from the visible world, murmured with fear and anger. The sickness it caused in his torso was vaguely familiar.

The drones whirred and throbbed with snapping sparks as they raced up through storm clouds full of ice and lightning. The billows churned in the pitch darkness, knocking them about, whipping and spinning them in sharp gusts, smashing a few against each other, taking out brothers before the battle had even begun. Kierkad avoided this, because of the drone's abilities not his own, and pierced the sky in as vertical a climb as he could achieve.

Cresting the height where the floats usually appeared, he began swooping in wide curves to the right and to the left, searching for them. Where were the sparkling shimmers that gave away their position? Where was the shower of flickerings, of reflections, of moving stars, that always guided them to their targets?

The Sentinels had improved their tactics against the Cascade—but the enemy had not wasted their time either.

They were dropping now at night—and were invisible.

It was a shock when he encountered his first float, flying into it and cutting it to shreds with barely a hint of vibration on his wings. He only knew it was there because the tiny chip that hung at the center of the float tapped onto his visuals, clung there for a moment, spitting out little showers of electronic data, and fell away in the wind.

It left the oddest impression. Like shapes or sounds or movements distilled into blips and blanks. He felt as though he should know…

No time.

The brothers were yelling and humming, sweeping through the skies with determination. They knew now that they were dealing with an unseen threat, and it revved up their drive to fight and conquer. Kierkad joined their cries and yells, rolling to one side, then the other, diving, curling, pulling up and chasing. There was a moment when the floats were sheered that they flashed a little spark and as the drones cut down more and more of them, the flashes became the guide to finding more. They fell in patterns. The more they sliced, the easier they were to track down.

At least until they had fallen low enough to enter the storm clouds and then it became a nightmare. Kier searched and dodged and flew in those clouds, narrowly missing other drones many times, till his hands ached, his body ached all over, and still the end wasn't called. Chip after chip had flicked onto his visuals and flashed its package of gibberish.

They fought all night till the hour before dawn and at that point, Kierkad was sure, some had touched the surface. The drones were barely fifteen meters above the ground.

He chased one down and yanked himself back into his body so he could track it. He was two kilometers away! He revved up the pod and sped to the site where he had last seen it. Three other pods and two brothers on foot arrived at the same time.

Someone was yelling to the people to stay indoors. It would be taken care of.

One brother reached it first and sliced it with his right hand… which didn't look like a hand. It was hard to tell in the dark. He fell onto one knee and picked up the chip. Another brother stretched out his hand and grabbed for it at the same time. Both of their hands touched it. One paused. The other crushed it between his fingertips.

The brothers all stood and stared at the dust that fell.

They just stopped and looked at it.

No one spoke.

Perhaps they all were tempted by the same question.

Were they fighting against nothing?

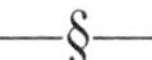

The two brothers appeared for the morning meal a few hours later, while all the others recovered in their bunks, immobilized in the sleeping pose they all assumed. Robots swept out carrying great trays with enough breakfast for the entire complement and deposited them around the room.

Kier placed himself at the seat farthest from the door where he could see all who came in and filled his plate with steaming food. When Seda joined him, he wasn't surprised.

"Day," Kier greeted.

"New day," Seda gave the customary reply, filling a plate and sitting across from him.

"Perhaps this morning the brothers are resting after last night," Kier suggested between bites.

"They sleep more deeply than we do." Seda lifted his eyes from his plate to look at him. The *person* was there, behind the eyes. Tired, bloodshot eyes.

"Yes."

Neither ate much.

"You had waking hours then?" Kier considered the words before he spoke them, not wanting to trigger the suppression of the Indoctriny.

"I slept for one hour and have not closed my eyes since."

The robots refilled their mugs of hot liquid. Kier stared down at it, puzzled. He hadn't been aware of drinking much less emptying his cup—but he must have. It felt interrupted, truncated, as if a few minutes had been snipped from the morning making a blankness in his memory.

"I slept until now and when I awoke, it was time to get up. This is reasonable." Kier held his mug and stared into it, watching the surface of the infusion ripple and the cloud rise.

"Did you see images in sleep?" Seda spat out carelessly before tossing a huge forkful of hash in his mouth. "Love this," he added, as though that were the thought that really mattered.

"I have never seen the homeland," Kier affirmed without breaking his fixation on the tea. Was it tea? It might be. The under layer, the part of himself that had torn away, was thinking and noticing; it had a different intent he couldn't follow, but he was aware of it. Kierkad was enjoying the comfort of the tea, smelling it, holding it in his hands, drinking it. "I like this tea."

"The tea is good," Seda picked up his cup but looked at Kier as he drank. "I had forgotten what it was."

Those words caught the attention of Kier's under-layer.

"I saw things…" Seda added.

I saw things… Kier, the layer underneath, knew this was significant. Kierkad assumed it was nothing.

"The battle was fierce, Brother," Kierkad agreed. "The storm made it harder. But we did not collide again."

"Images in my sleep kept me awake."

Kier lifted his eyes and locked them on Seda's. He saw the *person*, the inner part of Seda. "Of the homeland…" he whispered.

"Of lightning flashes and sparks," Seda said—his words stirred flickers and blips, streaks and gusts of storm wind in Kier's memory.

"The storm…" he said, blinking and clearing his vision.

"The etchings in electric code…" Seda uttered these words and dropping his cup, fell into a deep swoon, crumpling off the bench to the floor.

"You are weary, Brother," Kierkad said. "Let another take your shift and you sleep." Soon Seda was carried out and taken to his bunk for recovery.

Kierkad continued eating his breakfast and drinking his mug of warm liquid. It felt good. When he rose to his feet after he was done, he wavered for a moment. "Am I to work today?" he asked himself, "or is it nobler to replenish my sleep and be stronger tomorrow?" He didn't care which.

The compulsion would decide for him.

He snapped to attention and began marching for the door and his pod. *Work it is*, he thought. *Tonight, I will catch up on my sleep.*

In the under-layer, Kier noticed how the choice had been made for him and kept it in mind, wondering if it were significant.

Images in sleep. Was there such a thing? Some of the brothers had been known to speak of it. They used to talk about them at the morning meal. Images of the brothers, the work they did, of simple things, only it was different than the Harbor. The homeland, they said.

Kierkad never had them. *I have never had images in sleep*, the thought moved secretly in the under layer. *But then...have I?*

Flashes sparked in his mind, streaks of lightning, electronic code—only an instant, and it was gone. More than gone, it was forgotten.

Kierkad smiled with joy, surveyed his neighborhood, and began his first patrol of the day.

CHAPTER 4

11 Days

I have chosen this life
Indoctriny over strife
—14th chant, lines 6-7

No one besides the Sentinels ever entered the Harbor. This wasn't a law, but it might as well have been.

The massive base stretched out, black like charcoal against the river's warm, green banks and cool flowing waters, absorbing light and sound. Upstream, the town sprawled over the hills, brightly painted homes with white picket fences, leafy climbing trees, orchards, vineyards, gardens, and grassy yards. It was filled with the chorus of birds at dawn, children during the day, and crickets at dusk.

But if the music of the town was composed of the sounds of life, then the echoes in the Harbor were the somber tones of a tomb.

No alarms went off when a little figure moved along the riverbank and snuck through the grass up to the Harbor's exterior. It slunk around the edges until it reached the front entrance and then raced through the doors in a burst. Inside, it continued to press against the walls and creep on tiptoe down passageways and around corners.

Kier saw it in front of him where two passages intersected, when the child scampered across, arms flailing in a haphazard maneuver, tumbling but never falling. Stepping into the hallway, he looked for the child and found it pressed against the wall with its eyes closed, barely peeking through the cracked lids.

The child thought itself invisible, perhaps.

Kier stared right at it and for two breaths it remained immobile, then with a leap, it sped across the hallway and farther down to duck into a doorway where it paused and held its eyes closed again, peeping through its lashes.

The child believes it hasn't been detected, Kier decided, as he turned to walk toward it. Under the surface, he felt a hint of amusement and wondered at this new sensation. Why would he enjoy the child's shallow subterfuge and unsuccessful spying? On the surface of his mind, Kierkad decided the child needed assistance to return to its proper domain.

He intended to speak once he stood in front of the child but when he reached it, the strength of his under-thoughts resisted. Suppression didn't kick in right away, so he let the inner self rise to the surface. He searched the child's face for indicators of its intentions.

Flicker. The child opened one eye and squeezed it shut again when it noticed how close the Sentinel was, gritting its teeth with something like a grin… or a grimace of fear. It was hard to distinguish between the two.

"Are you lost?" Kier spoke to it softly.

The child peeked and closed its eyes again, still holding itself immobile against the closed door. It peeked again, shaped its mouth into a "no" and shook its head. Now it stared up at him, eyes wide with curiosity and daring.

Kier understood the courage it had taken to come in and found an almost instinctive bond with the little imp. To the child this was *fun*.

What had it come to find? he wondered.

"The Harbor is our home. Visitors never come," Kier explained quietly, wondering how a little misdemeanor such as this ought to be handled. There were no instructions in the code and no indications…

Suppression arose. The system had finally decided to observe the scene more closely and began to compel Kierkad to act.

"You are trespassing," he said in a more authoritative tone reaching a hand out to grasp the child's arm.

Slap! The child tapped his arm with a look of delight and a faint "Aha!" that it couldn't seem to repress and began to run.

Stop the child. Every Sentinel in the facility felt the unspoken command.

Kier gazed down at his arm and saw a square-shaped piece of metal, scratched with pencil lines, stuck to his sleeve. It looked familiar. His body rotated in obedience to the order it had been given but his mind dragged behind it.

It reminded him of a chip. A clumsy copy of the enemy's virus.

"Are you alone?" one of the Sentinels demanded of the child they had easily cornered, as more gathered behind him creating a wall of Sentinels, shoulder to shoulder in a corral around them.

"Yes," the child spoke clearly, though it panted for breath and its eyes darted around looking for escape.

Kier plucked at the chip as he drew close, tucking it out of sight into the seam of his sleeve, and joined ranks.

"Who sent you?"

"No!" it squeaked, shaking its head fiercely.

Another Sentinel made an attempt. "You have entered the Harbor without being summoned."

"Invited," another one amended.

"I'm not supposed to be here!" the child spread out its hands. "So, I'll just get out of your way. Right?"

"This one has come to us freely," another one said. "We welcome it."

"It has not come to us openly. We don't know its purpose."

Kier found the conversation strangely stilted. Why were they all speaking so mechanically? This wasn't what it was like when they were alone with each other. "Why have you come?" he found his own mouth uttering. Then he understood that the system itself was directing the conversation, something it rarely did. His under-layer quivered in revulsion.

"I'm leaving! Come on!" the child's voice began to waver, nearing a screech. "Let me go! I was just pretending! It's just a game!"

"What is a game?"

"You know, for fun!" it started pushing at one of the Sentinels, trying to squeeze between his legs, but he reached down and grabbed its arm causing it to howl.

The disorientation descended on Kier as forcefully as when his avatar and Seda's had collided. The wailing thing became alien and frightening. Several of the Sentinels shuddered and clenched their fists and he wondered if they were under the same compulsion.

"Stop screaming," the one holding it said.

"Let him go," Seda's voice broke through, solid and stable, anchoring Kier's mind. He turned his head and saw him, his hand resting on the arm of the brother who was holding the child. "You are hurting him."

Juravkad released his hold and looked Seda in the eyes. "I was not aware of this," he replied. "I am sorry, child," he added to the boy whose face had begun to display real fear.

"Stand back, Brothers," Seda began to reason with them. "We must allow the little one to leave without causing him any more trouble. The people we care for are sure to be looking for him."

Several stepped back. Others resisted and stared at him.

"They trust us," he said, and with that most of them began to move, opening a way for the child to flee—which he did, speeding at such a rate that Kier half expected to see little flames behind him.

Six of the brothers remained rigid in their positions glaring at Sedakad, as if they were made of iron.

"You are not in harmony," one of them said.

"I am in harmony," Seda responded calmly as he stepped closer to the one who had spoken. "you have misrepresented the Order to our flock because you are NOT in harmony. The outside entered and you neglected the robes of kindness we wear for them. YOU need a reset."

Kier expected to see Seda crumble under the system's discipline but to his surprise, the other six fell to their knees groaning, clasping their heads and stomachs.

The system had listened to Seda and agreed!

Seda turned to look at Kier who stood still nearby watching. "Brother?" he prompted, taking a step toward Kier. His eyes were strange, as if carrying several reflections at the same time and each one appealed to him in a different way.

The Sentinel in Seda tested Kier to see if he needed discipline. The brother in him looked for agreement, perhaps reassurance. Other shadows, flitting with hints of color unlike any seen in the Harbor, as though the outdoors were mirrored in his mind with hints of water and leaves and flowers— these groped toward Kier looking for…understanding.

He has an under-layer, the conviction pierced Kier's heart and jolted him in his inner thoughts. This was how he was able to think about the child when the rest of them were simply being controlled.

Kier's under-layer surged and flashed in his eyes with recognition, understanding, and concern for the danger Seda faced. *No, Brother!* he wished he could say, *Don't let them know!*

Seda gazed back at him, knowing what he meant. Or maybe not *knowing* exactly, but the link between them was real.

Kier remembered, *Eyes are the link*. It had never made sense before.

Seda wrestled with something he wanted to say, and Kier waited. They both knew how difficult it was to talk about…whatever it was they had learned. The Indoctriny was hard to work around but it was wedged inside them, fixed. The system in the Harbor, on the other hand, that governed and trained them at all times—it was actively engaged in identifying aberrant behavior or words.

Seda's eyebrows furrowed, and lips twisted as he tested words and chose not to say them. Finally, he spoke, and no punishment followed.

"One," he said.

That was all.

A smile and a nod were all he added as he turned and walked away.

Darkness filled the room where Kier lay stretched out on his back with his arms crossed over his chest. Opening his eyes, he could barely detect the outline of the walls around him. His arm was pressed over his heart, the mark of the Sentinels humming faintly with its own glow, warming the skin under his tunic.

He no longer found it comforting.

Rising to a sitting position without moving his legs, he lowered his arm slowly and watched as a faint light sparked from it before the symbol faded into blackness.

An image in his mind of the boy's chip had woken him, preventing him from resting. He let his thoughts roam over the memory he had made, fingering it, examining it closely, smelling and tasting it. There was nothing electronic about it, nothing harmful. There was no reason why it should be so jarring that he had been forced to sit up to consider it.

Turning his head, he looked at his suit, hanging on the wall in its usual spot. The little square piece of metal was still tucked into the seam of the sleeve, hidden. It was made only of flexible aluminum and the pencil etchings were crisscrossed lines. It was a toy, a child's plaything.

Yet it had been real enough to the boy to risk entering the Harbor to plant it on a Sentinel. Had he known of the danger?

What danger? Kier rotated to drop his legs over the side of his bed. The question troubled him. He *knew* there was danger, but why did he think that? What was the danger he felt and why was he so certain? Because he couldn't deny an absolute conviction of peril for any child who crossed that threshold.

Another thought that troubled him was that if the boy was pretending to plant a chip like the ones that fell in the Cascade—what kind of a game was that? Did he wish to harm the Sentinels? Did he view them as opponents? Was this reasonable for children?

As he rose to his feet, he sensed the Harbor system observing him. It had never mattered before, but this time, his under layer resented it, and it astonished him to notice how that feeling was untouched by the surface calm the system projected into him. He was getting stronger, more able to exist in two levels without being detected.

Dim lights activated. Kier scanned the room, noticing for the first time how barren it was, devoid of patterns or color or adornment of any kind. Blank walls. Stark floors. Cold and expressionless.

A Sentinel was one of many. Kier knew himself to be a distinct individual, but it was hard to see how he differed from any of the other brothers. Their thoughts, directed both by Indoctriny and the Harbor system, were parallel, if not identical. Their clothes, rooms, habits, speech, everything about them, were uniform and in sync.

Kier took two steps over to his armor and placed a hand over the breastplate, warming and lighting up the Sentinel symbol embedded in it. This was merely a ploy. He had often done it when he woke at night, before he had split, and it had become necessary to disguise his inner turbulence from the system. It vibrated under his palm as he continued to think.

If he could have found words to express his growing concern, they might have been: *Who am I? What am I apart from my task?*

He thought of the child. It would be a simple thing to conduct a mental data search for the boy's identity and to know whatever he wished about him— but a deep reluctance advised him against it. Better that the Harbor not know he was troubled, or if it knew, better not to reveal the cause.

Seda had persuaded the Harbor to let the boy go because others would miss him, and the Order of the Sentinels didn't want to lose the trust of the people. The child had a family. This conjured an image of humans of varying sizes holding hands, taking care of one another.

Why had the Harbor wanted to capture the boy? Only one Sentinel was needed to escort him back outside, but it had summoned *all* of them to surround him. What would have happened if it had decided to keep him?

Pain spread in his lower torso and the system responded with *calm*, forcefully imposed on his body, so heavy that he began to collapse on himself, crumbling to the floor. Then it drove him, half crawling, half dragging, back to his bed where he managed to pull himself up onto it and stretch out crookedly on his belly before he pitched into darkness.

The ache sunk deeper but did not fade while he was sleeping.

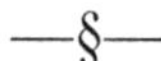

"Sentinels, to flight!" the voice of Pacificator Nirekad boomed through the halls. Kier had trouble making himself respond as the drugs inside him still coursed through his body. Blackness fought against the urgency of the need to obey the command.

Shoving sideways, he pushed himself off the bed and to his feet, gripping the edge as his head reeled. The room churned and tossed like a ship in a choppy sea. He groaned and shook, and a wave of cold sweat washed over him as he vomited onto the floor.

Restorators were at his side in minutes.

"We cannot dose him," he heard one state with a metallic twang.

"Agreed," another replied.

They lifted him onto the bed and quickly cleaned the mess he had left. The vertigo had taken over and he found himself reliving the moments in his drone as it dropped out of the sky after the mid-air crash. Over and over, he spun, whipped around, dropped at incredible velocity, never hitting the ground. Just falling, falling, falling.

Somewhere inside himself, part of him stood apart and observed, listening to the Restorators and noticing the anguish of his body. They were concerned as they opened panels on his thigh and in the middle of his back, checked numbers, and ran tests. He had never thought about those panels though he knew they were there. He wondered idly how much they had to do with governing him. Perhaps they managed the system's interaction with him. Or maybe they controlled the implants he assumed were in his frame.

"The Sentinel has reached the maximum level of allowed interventions," the one on his left determined.

"The system was operating outside of the safety parameters," the other replied.

Robotic units were well able to communicate digitally without creating sound waves. These words were obviously meant for his ears.

"The Sentinel must recover without intervention," the one on the left informed. A pause indicated it expected a reply, but not from the other Restorator.

"What must I do?" Kier prompted, surprised by the sound of his own voice; unsteady, unsure, higher pitched than normal. He didn't recognize himself and was repulsed at the sound of his weakness.

"Sleep, first," the one on the right side. "Then, take fluids. Soon you will be able to eat."

They sealed the panels and deftly rolled him over onto his back, laying his arms to rest for him across his torso.

"Your temperature controls are affected," the one on the left said.

"I will bring a covering," the one on the right submitted as it sped away.

Kier had never felt cold before in that room. He wondered what was happening and why, but the conditioning to never question resisted him. The word 'ill' came to mind, familiar as a concept, unknown as a memory: when the body can no longer maintain its functional equilibrium.

Was the boy's chip to blame?

There were many possible causes for his illness, invasion of foreign microscopic bodies or code, damage to the body, reduced power or nutrition supplies, electronic malfunction, mistreatment by the system…

The system was operating outside the safety parameters, the Restorator had said.

I knew that, he thought. He had sensed he was being 'managed' by the system a lot more in recent days than he had ever known before. It wasn't a distortion in his mind. Had it detected the split inside of him between the upper and lower layers? Or was it merely managing the behavior that deviated from standard Harbor system patterns?

If I'm being rectified, then so is Seda, he considered as he sank into the bed, trying not to shiver. A thick, bumpy cloth was spread over him as he closed his eyes, immediately warming his skin, taking longer to seep into the tissues. He wondered if Seda were ill as well.

Kier longed to sleep but the discomfort within his head and torso made it difficult. The Sentinel's resting pose, flat on the back with arms crossed over him, one forearm with the emblem pressed against his chest— made him ache. As he shifted onto his side and let the arm drop, he peered at the emblem.

It was dark and cold.

A wave of sorrow tumbled through him. Why would the system abandon him at this very moment? He knew it hadn't. He understood that the Restorators had turned off the connection so he wouldn't be automatically dosed and sent out. It was standard procedure. But he felt rejected. It was a strange and potent emotion.

As waves of dizziness and pain churned upward from his belly region and down from his head, he stared at the dark emblem, tracing its edges with a squinty gaze first, then a finger from his other hand. It was a wiry design pressed into the skin, flush with it, attached at a superficial, cellular level.

Barely thinking, eyes cracking heavily open and closed, back and forth, he began to pick at it with a fingernail. His mind wandered, almost drifting into sleep, then refocused, then dozed, and then woke. He scratched at it, grew still, then scratched again.

The skin separated from the edge with a stinging prick and a drop of blue beaded at the spot, followed by a ring of red around the droplet. He had confirmed what he wanted to know, though he didn't remember asking the question.

The emblem wasn't a part of him. It was merely added on.

Whether this meant something or not hardly mattered as the sleep he had been fighting took over.

CHAPTER 5

10 Days

"I have never counted before.
It seems such a sobering thing"
—Sedakad

Kierkad sat eating alone at a table in the mess. His stomach rumbled uneasily, and his head throbbed, oppressed by the lights. The warm porridge was soothing though it tasted of metal, and the hot beverage was likewise comforting. He held the cup close to his face and inhaled. The smell was familiar. Not because he drank it every day, but for some reason he couldn't pin down.

It means something, he thought, chasing the feeling and finding nothing to recall.

The brothers were out fighting and the play by play of their communications was being broadcast in the hall for him. Being outside the battle was a markedly different experience and this time was much worse than when he had crashed and had had to wait for a new avatar. There had been patrols to run then. This time, he was overcome by a sense of uselessness and defeat, as if he had failed his brothers when they needed him most.

"Searching…" several voices called out over each other, "searching… can't see…" The floats had become increasingly difficult to locate in the last few days as the enemy learned from each battle. Falling mostly at night, practically invisible, no longer in predictable patterns or nets, the Sentinels were increasingly frustrated in the goal of wiping them out before they hit the ground.

"A cluster!" someone yelled and a number of them hollered as they converged on the location to flame as many as they could. The noise was chaotic and confusing, but exciting to listen to. Kier lived it with them, remembering the motion of each dip and flurry of his drone. Sometimes a drone will vibrate in response to this, even if a Sentinel isn't in the pod. But not this time. The system was disconnected.

"Brother Kierkad," Pacificator Nirekad interrupted his focus speaking warmly, sitting across the table from him. He had a melodious voice, and he had pitched it to be kind, even paternal.

Kierkad smiled though the expression made his head hurt. "Master," he replied.

"You are afflicted with a bodily weakness," he began, raising his eyebrows. "Do not be alarmed by this."

His words stirred an unexpected emotional response, something like sorrow mixed with gratitude. Kierkad nodded and said nothing.

"The collision last week upset your equilibrium, and the system has been using chemical means to restore you," he explained. "However, it miscalculated and intervened too many times or perhaps, at inappropriate levels. I believe you have been informed of this."

"The Restorators mentioned it," Kierkad spoke, wishing he had kept silent as his voice resonated through his skull. He pressed the warm mug against his cheek.

"How is your mind?" the Pacificator asked.

It seemed a strange question. "My mind?" he whispered, looking into his master's eyes. What he saw there unnerved him. Unlike the system that merely watched and listened, the master examined his face and bore into his eyes with a gaze like a searchlight, plumbing the depths.

Kier steeled himself and smothered the panic that threatened to rise. He would hide the under-layer. He would guard his secret. He met the master's stare with one of his own.

"How is the Indoctriny? Does it care for you?" The intensity mounted as the master's eyes grew round.

"I am cared for," he answered automatically. He resisted the desire to be more persuasive.

"Are you loved?" Nirekad went on with his interrogation, glaring at Kierkad as if combing through his thoughts. The wildness in his face contrasted sharply with the calm in his body as he sat with hands folded on the table. Bulging knuckles, Kier noticed, graying hair, exaggerated brow, like an old man. He looked more human than Kier had ever detected before.

"I am loved…" Kierkad announced. "But," he added as his head pounded and he found himself gritting his teeth, "I am left behind. It is…" No word rose up to complete the sentence.

"Yes," Nirekad smiled showing his aging teeth. "I understand. I am allowed to remember that experience, for I was once one of the brothers. Now, I am more than that." He continued in his attempt to read Kierkad's mind.

Can he read my mind? Kier wondered. As soon as he had formed the thought, he was absolutely certain he could not. The master was looking for something out of reach of the system, but he was waiting for visual cues, tells, to give Kier away.

And he would get none.

"I have devoted my life to the noble cause," Kierkad said with true zeal, in spite of the pain in his head, in spite of the troubled under-layer. The words were true and held great significance for him. "I have laid aside all other endeavors for this. I love those I serve. And if I die in this service, I am satisfied with the life I have given. If I live and can no longer serve among the brothers…"

This took some thought because he had never been given a rote line for this possibility. "Then I will serve…" he went on slowly, testing the words, "… my brothers."

Nirekad's gaze readjusted to stare at him with recognition. "Yes, Brother," he uttered thoughtfully.

Kierkad ate several bites of his porridge, swallowing tentatively after each one. The warm drink had cooled but he sipped it anyway. The Pacificator watched patiently, almost as if he enjoyed the company and were reluctant to leave. All the wildness had faded from his countenance, leaving a frail shadow of a brother, almost humanlike, ruminating over old memories.

Kier felt the warmth of his company though it was superficial and made his inner loneliness more pronounced.

"When will I be reconnected to the system?" he asked as the food began to digest, and his pain began to diminish.

The Pacificator placed his left hand on his own right forearm over the place where no emblem was embedded, only an etched mark remained. It was an absentminded gesture, one he would never have indulged if he hadn't let his guard down. In that moment, Kier saw what he might become, and it terrified him. He had given up everything to become a Sentinel and to lose even that, to no longer belong to the brothers, would be a loss—a death—far greater than he could fathom.

Nirekad didn't see the flash of fear and Kier had it squelched before their eyes met again.

"You are eating and will soon be well," the master informed him, withdrawing into himself and reestablishing the distance he normally maintained from the Sentinels. "The system will be restored with some safeguards to prevent a reoccurrence of the blunder."

"Day," he added as he rose to his feet to walk away.

"New day," Kierkad replied.

—§—

The passage of time was an unnatural construct for Sentinels. They weren't given clocks or calendars and there were no vacations or festivals to break up the seasons. They had day and night—and that was all. For most, it was enough.

Kier had been satisfied with it for…before this day. But his memories were stored out of sequence, and he couldn't assemble a sense of length of time. The question, *How long?* wasn't even part of his experience. Conversation with humans was carefully guided to avoid time references and his mind had never seemed to need them before.

Now he craved them.

How long had he been a Sentinel? How long had he fought the Cascade? How long had he known Seda? How long would things continue as they were?

Life *today* had always been enough. The Harbor stored his memories for him and gave him a fresh start each morning. He was aware of progress and some changes in the battle with the floats, but he didn't have the tools to put together a story of how it had started, what had changed, and what it all meant. He had always assumed they were making headway against the onslaught and that the Sentinels would ultimately defeat them.

He had no judgment to lean on and no words to describe what he lacked.

In the late afternoon, his symptoms had calmed enough for Kier to be restless, so he donned his patrol suit and strode out to his pod, announcing as he stepped in that he was going on patrol. The Harbor made no attempt to intervene.

Soon he was walking the streets of the town, turning to the right and the left, nodding and smiling, sometimes waving at the people he saw. Overhead, the Sentinel avatars swooped and dived, chasing after floats like a colony of bats converging on a cloud of insects.

"Sentinel?" one man paused in his shoveling to look at him in amazement. "Are you patrolling?" He glanced at the sky and then back, full of concern.

Kier came to a standstill and looked into his eyes. He couldn't resist the impulse. Something in him longed to look into a human's face and *see*. Would the system observe what he was doing without the connection to the emblem?

The man's eyes filled with compassion. "Sentinel," he spoke more softly. "Are you well?"

"I have been ill, but now I am well." Kier stared at him clinging to the kindness in that gaze, unlike anything he had ever witnessed before.

"You aren't flying with your brothers," the man had propped the shovel on end and was leaning on the handle. For the first time, it occurred to Kier that the people rarely used advanced equipment, and he always saw them doing menial tasks any robot could perform. Why was that?

"How long…" Kier began, pausing as if the suppression would crush the words. Nothing happened. Could he ask this question? Would he be disciplined for it later? "Do you know me?" he chose instead.

"Yes, Sentinel," the man replied. "You patrol our neighborhood regularly."

"Other Sentinels patrol here as well."

"That is true." The man laid the shovel down and took a couple steps closer. He crossed his arms, not like a Sentinel's resting pose, but in a human way, tucking his hands into the crook of the opposing shoulder. It looked relaxed. "Several different ones each day, about… mmm, maybe every couple hours? I'm not sure about that. Last week, there was a break in the routine…"

"Last week?" Kier caught the phrase he knew he should ignore.

"When there was a crash..." the man lifted his head to the sky as if remembering the event.

"I crashed... last week," Kier answered. "How long ago was that?" He felt a strange sense of elation as he spoke these words without suppression kicking in. His heart began to race, and he didn't know how to slow it down on his own.

"Ten days ago," the man lowered his gaze to look into Kier's eyes again.

"I see," Kier answered as the human warmth in that gaze pierced his soul. He felt so hungry for whatever that look represented. He had no name for it.

The man talked about that day, the explosion mid-air of one of the drones, somewhere in the distance, over the barley fields, close enough to be seen with the naked eye. He and all the neighbors had run out to watch and some of them had gathered around the Sentinel as he climbed from his pod. "So that was you," he added. "I thought so. I told them I recognized you. Some people say no one can tell you guys apart, but I can." He grinned.

"What is your name?" Kier thought to ask.

"Caden," he said, reaching out a hand to shake.

Kier stared at it.

"It's generally customary to reach out your right hand and shake when someone offers it to you," Caden laughed. "Like this." He grasped Kier's hand and shook it.

Kier let his hand drop back to his side, but his fingers absorbed and retained the sensation of a human hand through his glove. "I am Kierkad," he responded.

"Glad to meet you, Kierkad," he nodded. "Another one of those -kads. You Sentinels don't have a lot of variety there, do you?"

A whisper of children's voices behind him grew louder and more distinct and Kier realized he had been hearing them for several moments. They were having an argument about something.

"Yes, I did," one insisted.

"No, Liar," the other snapped back.

"It was that one, I told you it was that one!" The first hissed more vehemently.

"Prove it! I dare you!" A scuffle ensued and Kier was certain they were wrestling on the ground.

Caden raised his voice a little, telling them to cut it out and stop fighting. And to stop interrupting while he was having a nice conversation with the Sentinel.

Kier turned around to look at the children. One of them was the boy who had snuck into the Harbor.

"I knew it was you!" the child said with glee, his eyes sparking with excitement.

"He's a liar," the other boy sneered. "He says he went into the Harbor."

Caden's face darkened. "Never do that, boys. Never go in there."

"What is your name?" Kier asked the boy who had not lied.

"See?" the second one said triumphantly. "I told you he was lying! He didn't go in there!"

"Grant," the boy's eyes widened as he got a good look at Kier. "It was you! Wasn't it? I knew it! I knew it!"

"Grant," Kier said, forming the name awkwardly as if it were forbidden to call children by their names—but it wasn't. There were no rules against. It just wasn't done. "You should not have gone in there."

"He WHAT?!" Caden burst out, his face turning red. It looked like anger, but his eyes were afraid. All of sudden Kierkad's visit became ominous. And not just in Caden's mind. The reaction was contagious, and Kier began to respond to it, hostility rising within him.

The second boy's mouth dropped open in astonishment.

Grant pursed his lips together in defiance. "I was looking for YOU and I found you. I can't say any more than that…"

Caden was terrified now and reached out to grab the boy to yank him away, to end the conversation as quickly as possible. But Kierkad extended an arm to block him and he froze, poised against the Sentinel's rigid limb.

"Why were you looking for me?" Kier wanted to know. Not the system. Not the Indoctriny. Not the Sentinels. "How did you know me and why…" What were the right words?

Caden let loose a low moan. "Sentinel, the boy is a child…he was playing…it's nothing…" Kier could feel the man's heart pounding against his arm, where he leaned against him.

"I've seen you around here lots of times. And you crashed and I knew it was you…" the boy showed no hint of alarm, oblivious to Caden's rising panic.

"You came into the Harbor looking for me specifically," Kier tested, taking a step toward him. With one sweeping gesture, he knelt on one knee, rested his left hand on the boy's shoulder, and shoved the man behind him. His right arm curved out to block him if he should try to reach the child.

"Yes," Grant said, as if he trusted Kier and was safe with him.

He was *not* safe with him. Kier didn't know why, but he didn't want the boy to trust him.

"You put a chip on my arm."

Grant's eyes bugged out and his mouth dropped open, delighted for an instant, followed by apprehension. "Uh…yeah…"

Caden moaned again, stepping forward, and was shoved back. Perhaps he was related. Maybe even the boy's father.

"Why do you want to destroy me?" Kier asked. He hadn't noticed his hand tightening on the boy's shoulder. He wasn't aware of the slowly contracting embrace he was trapping him in.

He didn't know his suit was darkening and a shadow was falling over his face.

Caden and Grant both screamed at the same time, the boy began thrashing and the man clung to the Sentinel's right arm crying out for mercy. The second child jumped onto his left arm, hanging from it and kicking; he was screaming too, demanding the Sentinel let go.

A great confusion arose within Kier and for a moment, the vertigo returned. The wailing of human voices, the thudding and pushing against his body, the spinning and nausea, all churned within him. With a guttural cry, he lurched backwards staggering, releasing the boy, knocking over the man, and tossing the second child.

Grant fell to his hands and knees weeping. "No, I don't…no, I wasn't…" he choked between sobs.

"I'm not able to…" Kier tried to salvage the debacle. "I can't…" He was nearly incapable of explaining himself. The system had always stepped in, and he had always submitted.

"Never go into the Harbor again," was all he able to put together.

"No, I won't," Grant gulped, rose to his feet and ran off, with Caden and the second boy close on his heels.

Kier found a tree to lean on and braced himself against it as he struggled to regain his composure. He could tell now that his body armor had darkened and watched as it grew light again. What did it mean?

Why had it darkened? Was it responding to his inner reactions? Or was it being controlled by the Harbor through a different access point?

How long have I lived with this curse? Was the question that haunted him as he turned abruptly and headed back to the Harbor.

"I am not fully recovered," he announced on his return and the Restorators rushed to his aid. Food and rest helped the body, but nothing touched the anguish of the under-layer.

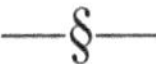

The parameters for Kier's oversight changed. After he recovered from his illness and had been reconnected to the Harbor system, he noticed the emblem glowed and hummed differently. At night when he should have been sleeping, he lay awake and thought about the change. He had more freedom to speak now and was no longer subjected to heavy dosing or overwhelming suggestions. To counterbalance it, he was assigned to daily Indoctriny refreshers in the cells along the south wall where he was led in drills and tests reinforcing all the principles he had been taught. He answered scenarios, quoted passages, played games of mental skill.

"Remember," the program always wrapped up with, "You are noble."

"I am noble," he would repeat.

"You are valuable," it would add.

"I am valuable," he would echo.

"You are loved," it would finish triumphantly.

"I am loved," he would parrot back—but he no longer believed it.

The emblem had always been a symbol of love for him. There was something personal and comforting about it. But that connection had been altered and his confidence in his place among the brothers had changed along with it. He wasn't an integral part of the moving, breathing, beautiful system, the brotherhood of peers joined by a common zeal, the shared calling. He was an easily unhitched periphery, dangling from the Harbor network, at the mercy of its benevolence.

Now the mark of the Sentinel symbolized his insignificance. Just as the corner he had picked at could be loosened from his skin, Kier, too, could be detached from the Harbor. The fact that the system had never noticed or repaired the imperfection amplified the message.

He may be noble. But valuable? He wasn't convinced. And loved?

He was not.

CHAPTER 6

9 Days

"The heart peers through the eyes.
Watch as well as listen."
—overheard on patrol

The Cascade fell six times in four neighboring places, cycling from one location to the next, then beginning the round again, and the Sentinels were forced to fight for long stretches without breaks for meals or rest. Never had they been sent out for so long without reprieve before, as if there were no reinforcements. As if the Sentinel bases across the valleys were unable to support one another.

As if the war were being lost.

Stumbling into the Harbor after fourteen hours of battle left Kier delirious with fevered thirst. Other brothers had managed better, but then they had the benefit of full Harbor support, with chems and measured sustenance during flights.

He had to make his own way to Restoration. Two brothers lay on cots there, unconscious and unmoving. Murukad and Gerenkad. Kier realized these were recent additions to their number, replacements, and they were clearly inexperienced in battle. Bruises around their faces and limbs showed where they had thrashed in the pod as they flew their avatars.

"Sentinel," one of the Restorators approached him. "You must go to the mess hall and drink first. Then eat. A unit will meet you at lavage to teach you self-cleansing and then you must sleep. This will now be your personal regimen."

"I have never attended to my own…fatigue…before," he responded, wondering if that was the right word. He continued to stare at the Sentinels lying nearby, fascinated by the flurry of activity around them as tubes were attached and oblong sheaths rolled over each one to seal them into healer cells. *How many times have I been treated in one of those?* he wondered.

"Your progress in the Order calls for new training," the Restorator reminded him.

Kier turned and walked out again, guiding himself with one hand on the wall for balance. Weariness made the path to the mess longer than it had ever been before. *Before now*, he thought. In the past, it had been quicker. *Time is moving in a line, and I am beginning to remember the changes in sequence.*

Landing heavily on a bench across from Seda, Kier reached out for a pitcher of liquid, filled a tumbler, and drank it one guzzle. The water tasted clean and cool. Pouring another glass, he glanced at his brother—his friend. "I am thirsty," he explained.

"I can see that," Seda answered. "I expected you here sooner. It's been a difficult day."

"I needed healing but was not greeted by the Restorators, so I went to their station." Kier took another swallow. "I am progressing in the Order and require different training now." Setting the glass down, he let his shoulders sag. His whole body drooped, leaning over onto the table, as if almost every muscle were growing slack.

"I am also progressing," Seda nodded and began to scoop the dark colored stew in his bowl into his mouth. "But I think my regimen is different than yours. I have not been turned away at the clinic." He was exhausted too.

"I am…" Kier wanted to discuss suppression and how he had not sensed it for two days. And he wanted to talk about the passing of time and how memory has a progression, an order. But he hesitated.

"You are…?" Seda smiled vaguely between bites.

"I can speak of things I never used to care about," he ventured. If the system was listening, he could no longer tell. Food was placed before him, and he began to eat.

"I can think of many things I didn't used to notice," Seda's words brought no heaviness, but a hush fell over the room.

The mess hall was full of Sentinels, and they had all been talking, eating, and laughing; clanking bowls and spoons, sloshing water, scraping chairs and jostling tables.

All grew still.

"What do you mean?" Kier asked, though he worried about the quiet in the room and all the brothers who had dropped their heads to stare at their meals.

And he worried about the Harbor, watching and listening all the time, looking for aberrations that might disturb the cohesion of the group. If he could not be chemically manipulated, how would he be corrected when the need arose?

"Music, Kierkad," Seda replied. "I heard it on patrol, and I was aware of it. I have heard it before. People talk of emotions, and they share them with sound. I could hear those sounds."

Music began to play in the mess hall. Powerful, deep, long sounds, accented by rhythmic short ones, rising and falling, ebbing and flowing. Murmuring stirred among the brothers, and they began to talk and make noise again.

"We are familiar with this," Kier offered. But his eyes said something else. *I know you mean more than you are saying*, he was thinking.

Seda stared at him and caught the deeper layer in his gaze. Slowly he nodded and sadness filled his eyes. "There is a number I can't understand," he whispered, "but it agitates me in my belly and in my thoughts at night, when pictures and images flit through my sleeping mind."

"The number one?" Kier remembered he had said that. A serving bot refilled his bowl and he realized he was eating quickly in very large mouthfuls.

"No," Seda shook his head somberly. "Three."

"Three," Kier echoed between bites.

"It's a terrible thing, Kier." His eyes grew damp and bloodshot. "I don't know why, but I find it the most horrible integer I've ever known."

"Brother," Kier reached an arm across the table to grip his shoulder. "We are not alone." This was the appropriate brotherly response and should have been reassuring.

"Aren't we?" Seda challenged.

Piercing and ringing, the question entered Kier's chest and shook him to his core.

He could not deny it.

The skies were laden with storm clouds, and the darkness was oppressive. Flying through them, dodging to the right and to the left in measured sweeps, Kier searched for floats. Avoiding other drones depended more than ever on instruments and the Harbor system's backing. He could see nothing.

"Searching… searching…" came the cry from each of them on cue, confirming status and location every few seconds. This latest attack by the Cascade, dropping a short distance from the Harbor, was being countered by only twenty-seven Sentinels. Others were covering nearby regions or under treatment in the Restoration clinic.

A burst of flame on his starboard wing sparked a loud cry from Kier's lips. "Float!" he yelled, banking deeply to the right to chase its trajectory. Tiny sizzles crackled on the wing edges as first the float tissue, and then the chip, disintegrated. He sliced through the tempest, rain sheeting against the glass over his visuals, washing away the remnants.

Every Cascade attack engaged a new pattern, and it took a number of encounters before enough floats had been identified, and the system could deduce the tactics. When this happened, the drones could latch onto the design and plot a flight plan along its lines, slicing through floats all the way. It was an exhilarating experience.

"Cascade Tactical Pattern Extrapolated," the system announced, and Kier hollered as it spread across his visor. An elliptical spiral heading earthward, expanding in size as it neared the ground, and he was the first in the path. He accelerated, spiraling in an ever-wider swathe, flaming floats along the way, catching wisps of paper-thin fabric that would soon whip away in the wind, and snagging chips spitting flashes of data like sputtering fireworks as they extinguished.

Alarms sounded. He was approaching the surface. Withdrawing his consciousness from the avatar, he set it to auto-land and extracted himself from the pod. Gusts of wind tore at him at he ran along the pattern still traced in his visor heading for the nearest wisp, as floats that touched down were called. Lightning cut the sky and rumbling crashes followed almost immediately. Too close even for a Sentinel.

Apart from the split-second shocks of day-strength light, rending the clouds every few moments, the night was thick and impenetrable. Infra-red gave him enough clarity to detect surfaces and obstacles, to avoid hurling headlong, but movement was lumbering and awkward. He reveled in the realization that no other brothers were near, and he would be the one to demolish the viral units.

Kier found himself laughing. The storm, the bursts of heavy wind shoving him, almost lifting him from his feet, the ear-shattering thunder and the sky-wide etchings of untamed, unleashed electricity, the noise and chaos, the chase and the assurance of winning. They exhilarated him.

There! A crumple of grayish tissue lay sodden on the grass. With a leap, he was upon it, tearing back the cloth to find the chip underneath. Barking a wordless shout, he gripped it in his fingertips and lifted it eye level, smiling widely.

"Anarchy, be damned," he gloated, his voice lost in the storm, "Order has come upon you." And with a deft twist of his fingers, he smashed it to pieces. The thrill of conquest lasted barely an instant and immediately he hungered for more.

Five times he gained the privilege of crushing the Cascade's device and each time the pleasure was more fleeting than before. There was no Harbor involvement to extend or smooth his satisfaction. No stabilizer to govern his sense of accomplishment.

A dark mood fell on him, and he began to growl and murmur as he searched, wrestling with the thought that had taunted him a few times before, that he was a pawn in a cruel game and the great war being fought with an elusive enemy was nothing more than a mockery of true guardianship.

It was a relief to encounter other Sentinels along the path and continue the search together. They were able to maintain their stability and sense of purpose, and working with them accelerated the progress.

One incident, though, would come back to haunt him. The last wisp had fallen very near Caden's home and when he picked up the chip—which he insisted on retrieving, as if it were his right, and other three had given way without question—when he lifted it to his eyes, it flashed its digital trash at him. It spat its contradictory code, images, shapes, and equations at his head. And for an instant, he saw a room, a place, and was stirred to search for it, perhaps in this very house where he now stood on the lawn.

His gaze drifted to the house, took in the darkened windows, the locked door. Trees thrashed their branches and swings banged against each other in the yard. He pictured opening the door, walking down the hall, finding the room…and then, he didn't know.

The boy knew.

He looked at the chip again. The other Sentinels were yelling at him, trying to be heard over the wind. He should have heard them through his helmet, but the radio didn't seem to be working. One of them leaned toward him and cupped his hand over Kier's, forcing his fingers to close, pulverizing the little piece of metal.

Etched metal. Scratched with lines. Like the sound of crayons on paper.

Audio returned and he heard the final calls as the last wisp of the night was destroyed. Several voices were talking to him and to each other, but he made no answer. He just followed as they returned to their pods to coast back to base.

Kier searched for Seda as soon as he arrived, bypassing standard post-fight procedure.

He found Seda in his room, standing next to his bed, gripping the edges with his hands, still fully garbed in armor. There were smears and dirt all over it. The suit itself was darker than its normal silvery hue and different limbs seemed to be different shades of brown and copper, and some were gray, some green. The streaks and filth on it struck Kier as offensive somehow.

"You should not enter your room without cleansing," he reprimanded, though he himself had bypassed the lavage chambers to find his friend.

Seda turned his head and lifted a face of horror to him. Never had Kier seen such anguish in a Sentinel's eyes before. Puffiness around the eyes, jaw hanging open with the lips curving down, the stark distress that emanated almost palpably from it astonished Kier.

"Seda," he gasped. "What happened?" He took a step closer, and his brother straightened and turned to face him, holding his arms out on either side. There were deep gashes in the armor panels of his arms. They were cracked, with hanging shards, and bare skin was visible through the gaps. The Harbor's emblem throbbed in bluish purple through the opening on his right arm. And the larger emblem on his chest-plate pulsed in time to it. The darkest hues of the armor centered around those gashes.

Seda uttered a long wail. "Four!" he cried at last. "Kierkad, I am undone!! Now I know! I know what I…" With a great shriek he fell to his knees, clutching and shaking his head. "No! No!" he yelled over and over. "I must say it!"

But he could not say what he wanted. The Harbor was too strong for him. He collapsed on the floor and the Restorators arrived almost before he had landed. Ignoring Kier, they sped away with him, to cleanse, tend, and restore him to equilibrium.

Kier made his own way to the lavage chambers and followed the routine that they all required after a late-night skirmish. Lights dimmed all over the Harbor as the Sentinels went to sleep, laying peacefully in their cots, on their backs, arms folded across their torsos with the emblem on the forearm pressed against their chests. Silence reigned and the Harbor processed, compiling the news of the day, evaluating the current status of the Order, and making small adjustments to ensure future stability.

Kier lay still but was wide awake. The emblem pressed against his chest did not hum and gave off no warmth. His heart was thumping hard and exerting more pressure than he liked, and he kept thinking of Seda's words and his agonizing cry. What could it mean? What had happened? He nearly forgot his own experience with the chip and the image of a room. When it came to mind, he dismissed it. It seemed foolish now.

Seda had been counting. But what did it mean?

When he had begun to count, he had been pleased to find a word for his inner thoughts. "One," he had said, and that was enough to relieve the burden inside him. Had he counted to two? Kier couldn't remember. Maybe Seda had told him that number, and he had been distracted or didn't hear or didn't care enough to retain it. But when he reached the number three, Seda was beginning to be concerned. Something about it troubled him.

Have I ever counted? Kier wasn't including Math. They were all trained in highly advanced mathematics which they never seemed to use. It maintained a certain level of brain function that the Harbor considered optimal. But counting had always been an impersonal automatic system function. Counting groups of people, counting floats, counting... He couldn't come up with any other examples of counts.

Four of *something* had impacted Seda.

Sleep finally descended, bringing vivid dreams of wisps and chips, lightning and thunder, storm and rain. He felt the gusts of wind, savored the victory over each chip, always counting to four as he captured and crushed them, then starting over at 'one' with the next. They grew into a marching tempo, in counts of four. He found himself laughing and just as quickly crying. But it wasn't his voice weeping. It was Seda's. It was in the distance, wafting to him on the wind. He ran toward it, calling to him, and his words were snatched away in the squall. The beat went on, his fingers snapping to it, little specks of dust falling from them as he smashed the chips in time to it. *One. Two. Three. Four.* Where was his friend?

Down long black streets, across fields and streams, over boulders and into gullies, climbing trees, jumping pools of mud, the pace picked up and he raced like the wind. *Where are you?* he called every so often. No one answered. Only the moaning, crying, wavering voice, growing weary. Giving up. Till it was silent.

Even the wind died down. The thunder ceased and the rain slowed to a drizzle. He was walking, covered with mud, dripping, still snapping his fingers to a four/four meter, patrolling his normal route in the twilight before dawn. Then the voice picked up again. *Kier*, it said. *I'm here.*

The house. Without hesitating, he strode to the front door, pulled it open, rushed through the darkness to another door and entered a room... the room... and a child was there, sitting on the floor talking to itself.

Kier stood in the doorway, still snapping, still crumbling chips with his fingers, still counting to four. He heard the moaning voice again, and realized it vibrated in his own chest. He looked down at his arms where they lay crossed over himself in the Sentinel's resting pose, and the emblem on his arm glowed fire-red. It throbbed and ached like an infected wound. Groans were coming from his lips. *The voice is mine*, he thought, without emotion.

The child's chatter caught his attention again and he noticed it was leaning over paper and scratching away at it—drawing, coloring with crayons. Orange and green, black and purple, red, and more red. Kier reached out his burning arm, nearly blinded by the blazing molten red of the emblem and grasped the sheet.

The child turned to look at him. Eyes staring into his eyes. *The link is in the eyes*, he told himself, but he could find no understanding between them. Dropping his gaze to the paper, he saw the picture and recognized it.

It bore a fumbling image of a child cowering under a terrifying creature with jagged limbs. Other people running away. It was the picture he had once found and kept. And he moaned again. *What did it mean?*

Looking at the child, the eyes boring into his, he suddenly had a link and understood the thought in its gaze.

You know, it was telling him. You know what this means.

And he knew he should—but he didn't.

CASCADE

CHAPTER 7

6 Days

> *"If I should fall to rise no more*
> *As many comrades did before*
> *Then ask the fifes and drums to play*
> *Over the hills and far away"*
> —*Old Ballad, before the Severance*

The morning dawned thick and heavy as if the air were laden with dust, which it wasn't. Fog, so thick you couldn't see twenty meters ahead, blanketed the streets. Kier pressed through it, shoving his legs and arms in the customary marching stride, as if he were moving through sludge. The reoccurring nightmare was wrecking his rest at night, sapping him of strength, leaving him near despair. The Harbor had maintained his contentment at a specific level for so long, he was ill-prepared to manage it on his own.

As he neared each house, the lights in the windows became visible, but were quickly swallowed in the mist again, leaving him to his inner misery. The chill, perceptible at certain places on his body, hands, feet, exposed skin around the neck, was also unfamiliar and extremely unpleasant.

One home he passed had music playing on a device and he could see several people seated at a table, breakfasting together. Another had figures moving around inside, speaking in drowsy murmuring tones. Others showed people reading, or rushing about grabbing things, or were dark and silent with sleeping inhabitants. He wondered what each one's task for the day would be. Tapping into data as he passed their homes, he noted they had jobs and school, social commitments and hobbies, chores and outings. This one worked at a bank and golfed in his spare time. That family was preparing for a ski trip. This other one was overcommitted to activities, sports, meetings, volunteering, music lessons. The variety and also the similarity between them all mesmerized him.

It relieved him to think of them and not himself, but it amplified his isolation.

Seda had been mended imperfectly, if that was the right term. The damaged pieces of his armor were refurbished while the injured portions of his mind were patched and medicated. He no longer talked to Kier about anything. Mealtime lost its appeal without his companionship, and training sessions became a burden. Sedakad had lost the will to interact with anyone, and his face was habitually devoid of all expression.

Kier mourned the loss.

Every battle brought new casualties, Sentinels going out to fight and returning fewer in number.

CASCADE

Excellence in form and level of training had little bearing on the toll. No one could predict who would be next. Every morning as the list of names was read, all those lost in the region, from all the bases in the battalion, the brothers would listen and murmur their regrets. They spoke of the noble cause and bolstered one another's courage. They went out into the day with renewed hope and confidence, ready to lay down their lives for the Order.

Replacements no longer came in promptly. Kier had noticed that the Harbor's complement had been reduced to 72 and pairing for harmony and training had been adjusted accordingly. Patrols were shuffled to cover the lack. And battles were less likely to bring in back-up from other bases.

Sentinels were being wiped out far faster than they were being replaced, perhaps all over the Earth.

He thought about the planet as he plunged through the fog, nodding to the occasional person out for a run or walking to work. He and his brothers had been guarding the Earth for a while now. The Severance had not returned, at least not in enough force for the Harbor to be activated in defense.

How long has it been? he wondered. *How long have I lived here watching over the people?* He couldn't remember any other life. He tested some numbers. *One year?* he asked himself. *Twenty years? Two months?* None of it meant anything to him. The only time frame that made sense to him was the number of days since he had split inside. Eight days. Everything before that was a stationary chunk of existence without contour.

In his former existence, the one he had abandoned for the Noble Call, he may have lived in a home, had a job, eaten breakfast with other people…

this was the wrong train of thought to follow. He found himself yanked into a waking memory of the horrible dream, the dark hallway, the child in the room, the picture colored in crayon, the eyes. He broke into a cold sweat and found himself gasping for air for an instant, waiting for the Harbor system to calm him down.

But no stabilizers came to his aid. He was at the mercy of the image bearing down on his mind. "Ah…" his mouth gaping, he clutched at the emblem on his chest-plate. It shone and pulsed with warm yellow light, soothing, humming, but the attempt was futile, it went no deeper than the skin.

A man approached him tentatively and laid on hand on his shoulder. "Sentinel," he said. "You are in distress." He was dressed in a warm coat, a briefcase in his hand, clearly on his way to work.

Kier didn't want him to worry and meant to explain that he was fine, that the man could move on, but it wasn't true. And he couldn't find a way to say the lying words. He looked into the man's face and panted, fighting the pressure in his lungs. "I…" he searched for something to add.

"What is your name, Sentinel?" the man nodded, offering him something to say. He was a doctor, Kier noticed in the scan he accessed mentally.

"Kierkad," he responded without a clue as to what should follow.

"Kierkad, I don't know a lot about Sentinels," he explained, patting the shoulder he had touched. The motion, vibrating through the armor to his actual shoulder, was oddly reassuring. "But you were chosen for this… Noble Call, partly because of your similarity to us… if, that is… I hope that isn't offensive to you. I don't mean to minimize your importance or value to us…" He waited for a moment, but Kier merely looked at him. "The fact is, Kierkad, that you appear to be under some form of anxiety—at least, it looks like human anxiety. Maybe it's something different, but should you be patrolling right now? Is there some malfunction the Harbor needs to address?"

He waited, patting his shoulder, watching him thoughtfully. "Perhaps, you should take some deep breaths, exhaling slowly… yes, like that."

Kier began to calm down. The presence of the man, his voice, his hand tapping, all served to drive the nightmare away. "I see," he said finally, straightening and pulling away slightly so the man could no longer pat him. "You are correct in saying that I am in need of adjustments. This planet is difficult for us." He was able to state this because it was part of the Indoctriny and deeply ingrained, but the under-layer resented it. Subterfuge to avoid speaking the actual truth cut him off—cruelly so, from a human who was helping him.

It ended the brief interaction.

Something hardened in the man's face. Kier's expression was stone-like as well. He turned and continued his patrol without so much as a thank you.

"It's appalling what they're doing," he heard the man muttering behind him, "not even basic…drugs… poorly managed…"

For the first time, he wished that he could go back to the time before the split, when life had been solid and stable, when the world had been dull but safe.

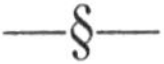

The late afternoon brought a swarm of floats around the region. Every base was activated at the same time, and the Sentinels were unable to cover the extent of the onslaught. Alarms that summoned the brothers to flight would cease once the required numbers were met but this time the horns continued blasting throughout the Harbor chambers for hours.

Kier welcomed the interruption of the training for the day. He had sought out Seda and found sparring with him to be a disappointment. Seda's every movement was precisely timed and in sync with the exercise, but his strength was tethered and flimsy. Kier had to restrict the power of his movements as if he were fighting a fern.

He had tried speaking. "What have you, Seda?" he had hazarded. "Are you…still counting?" The words were sandwiched in between blows and his friend had seemed unaware of them. "Have you…reached the…number five?"

'NEVER!!" Seda had roared suddenly, slamming him with a punch that had lifted him off his feet and projected him backward into the wall. Rage had disfigured Seda's face. His mouth had dropped open and the hand that had given the blow had hung limply at his side. Kier had fallen to his knees, the wind knocked out of him, groaning from the shock more than the pain.

Then the siren calls to battle had gone off and Seda had run from the room without looking back. Kier had taken longer to get to his feet, don his armor, and make his way to the pod, his torso aching as he walked.

He settled his pod under the shade of a massive tree near the park and paused for a moment to take in the rustling of the branches and twinkling of distant lights reflecting in the lake. With the heavy bank of clouds overhead, it was murkier than twilight though hours remained till sunset. And the morning's chill hadn't lifted. He breathed and focused on exhaling slowly.

Earth is beautiful, he thought. *Perhaps my world had a similar beauty and that's why this one is comforting.* The urgency to get out and fight seemed to have left him, though he could hear the voices of his brothers calling out and felt the impulse to engage a high adrenaline kick. The system, stripped of its power to dominate him, tried to rule him still. The pulse in his chest-plate grew stronger and the emblem on his arm echoed the frequency.

He understood the message but didn't care. He would move in a moment. He just wasn't ready yet.

But the Harbor system had other tools besides meds. A sharp jolt of electricity jarred him in his seat, leaving all his nerves aching and raw. The consequent flush of fear and alarm were systemic, generated by his own body, leaving him shaking and trembling all over. He gripped the control stick and plugged into the drone, groping with his mind to find it where it waited on top of his pod.

Taking off under a tree required some low flying and there were obstacles to swing around, which might have been enjoyable if he hadn't just been shocked. His nerves were on edge and his reflexes twitchy. Getting elevation proved harder than it should have. The system would know electric jolts would hinder his ability to fight but in weighing the options had probably decided losing his obedience was worse.

"Found a stream! Found a stream!" someone was yelling. "Slicing down a line of them... wait! Wait! They're scattering! Like they have... Woah!!" The shouts and cries of the Sentinels burst over each other, obliterating all meaning, but Kier could see what was happening by now. The floats were moving, not just with the wind or gravity, they spread out in different directions as if with a mind of their own—or a means of propulsion. If it weren't for the murky light still filtering through the billows overhead, it would be impossible to know where they were.

The Cascade had finally mastered every recourse the Sentinels had to find them in the air. Now most of the battle would have to be fought on the ground. Kier backed out of the avatar, returned to his pod relocate nearer the Cascade, and climbed out to search on foot.

"Engage laser to wipe out wisps," the system broadcast to the Sentinels, causing concern among a number of them. There would be some danger to the humans. It was unwise. But many of them obeyed immediately, engaging their guns, and Kier could see little flashes of light here and there as they blasted the targets.

He followed suit, pulling the laser from the casing at his thigh, ready to shoot, and scanning right and left with his infra-red, he searched for wisps. There, *sscctttsss…* and another, *sscctttsss…* he took out several of them without coming near enough to any homes to worry. Once he reached sidewalks and residential streets, though, he slipped the gun back into its holster.

A few more were easily crushed between his fingers, and he steeled himself to avoid counting them. He intentionally walked in an uneven pattern, avoiding the marching tempo of his dream.

I am Noble, he muttered under his breath, keeping his mind focused on the task at hand. *With noble goal we walk the streets…with noble heart we uphold peace…with noble zeal we combat threats…. All storms of war will cease.* The chant helped.

Screams. Crashes. Sounds of wood and walls breaking.

Kierkad leapt forward as the noise rolled down the street, hurtling himself over fallen branches, refuse of the morning storm, fallen wisps, a discarded bicycle, and everything else in his path. Racing. Rounding a corner, he homed in on the tumult taking place at a house halfway down the block. Some people were running away, shrieking. Others were running toward the scene. Glass shattering marked the blackening of the interior of the building as the lights went out and thumps, shouts, and a terrible racket boomed out the doorway. The door itself was ripped off the hinges, broken in pieces on the front porch.

Kier knocked people aside as he sped up the lawn and through the gaping hole. Scuffling and muffled screams continued, some high pitched, some lower, leading him down the short passageway. A closed door blocked access to source of the bedlam. He threw himself against it twice and the second blow knocked it open leaving him to tumble in and slip to his knees on the floor.

Silence fell abruptly.

A faint, distorted shape, recognizable and memorable, glowed gently in the pitch black of the room, its yellow light fading till it began to flicker out, growing cooler and bluer with each oscillation. Finally, it burnt out altogether.

Kier rose to his feet, fumbled for his emergency light, and clicked it on. Turning, he scanned the room, trying to make sense of it. Overturned furniture, boxes with the contents dumped, a busted chair, shards of glass, piles of wadded clothes, a mattress flipped off the side of a bedframe that was collapsed onto the floor at one end.

Someone flipped on the lights. Now he could see the blood. It was smeared on handles, corners, edges, small amounts everywhere. As if humans had been fighting and giving each other a terrible beating, leaving traces of their wounds with each kick and wallop. People behind him in the hallway stared but an eerie quiet reigned.

Who had been fighting and where were they now?

Kier walked around the room over the tumble of junk, kicking things aside, pushing things out of the way, looking for a clue, something to make sense of it all. The window on the opposite wall was missing. Had they fled through there? Had they panicked when he pounded on the door and gotten out just before he got through? Maybe he could have even seen them if he had turned his emergency light on first.

"Who was fighting?" he asked the people still standing at the door as he continued to search the room.

"We don't know, Sentinel," someone said, choosing to speak for those gathered behind him. "We're just as shocked as you are." The woman's voice wavered with fear. He glanced at her and detected it. He saw both the fright the room induced and the courage she countered it with to stay and look and speak.

Kier remembered the glowing image he had seen before the lights came on and made his way to that part of the room. It must have come from the pile of blankets or laundry on the floor. He dug through it, tossing pieces of cloth aside.

The woman let out an ear-splitting scream when he found it, scrambling backwards, bumping into people as she fled. Others pressed in taking her place, straining to see what he had found.

The emblem of the Sentinel, twisted and misshapen, hung loosely from strings of flesh, tangled in a wad of blood-soaked clothes. It was framed in fragments of dark brown and copper colored metal, in thick shattered chunks that glistened in the light. He gripped the whole thing and straightened, holding it up in the light.

It was armor, the piece that covered the right forearm. Broken in multiple places, cracked and sliced open, dripping in blood. Inside it was a remnant of the arm that had used it.

He knew. There was no need to wait for the system's analysis. As he stared at the mutilated thing, tracing its jagged edges with his eyes, he saw where the armor had been cracked before, then repaired. He knew beyond a shadow of a doubt whose arm it had belonged to.

Turning around to look at the people, he noticed for the first time that his own armor was changing color. It was growing darker, as if danger detected meant enemy discovered!

No! he commanded within himself. *I am Noble! I am here to guard this flock!* And he resisted the conditioning of Indoctriny that insisted he defend himself as a Sentinel. Gritting his teeth, he willed the system to reverse the programmed response—and it did.

People were backing away from him as he stepped forward. Spellbound, horrified, confused, unable to look away. "What will happen?" someone called out to him.

"Oh, no!" he heard another voice wailing somewhere outside. "It's happening again! It's too much! It's too much!" They scattered as he advanced carrying his brother's arm-plate and made his way outside. All around neighbors, assembled to view the source of the ruckus, gawked at him.

In the distance, he could hear and see the Sentinels sweeping the ground for wisps, extinguishing them with lasers or crushing them in their fingers. He wondered if there were others who would be taken down before it was over.

Kier raised his head to look into the darkening skies where the clouds were finally parting, and a few twinkling stars were showing themselves. *What power*, he wrestled inside, *was so great that a brother could be snatched away like that?* Somehow, it had tossed aside the Sentinel's link to the Harbor then yanked the defender away without a sound. *Without a sound!!*

He walked down the path to the sidewalk and headed slowly back to his pod. Before he had gone a few paces, he reached a wisp. How harmless it looked!

"How is this a threat to us?" he asked aloud without thinking. Bending over, he found the chip buried in the cloth and picked it up with his free hand. He straightened and brought it close to his face. He remembered the boy's piece of metal that he had planted on him. Kier had looked at the toy in this way and tasted it. Then he had hidden it.

For an instant, he considered hiding this one, tucking it into his armor somewhere, saving it to ponder later. And he thought about tasting it. But his face shield was fully engaged, and his gloves were stained with blood.

Seda's blood.

He crushed the chip and let the dust scatter, a great sorrow filling his heart.

And he counted from one to four in time to his footsteps.

CASCADE

Chapter 8

5 Days

Music speaks when words cannot.
—Banner on the school wall

Six hours in Restoration was what it took to reset Kierkad. He was aware of every hour, every minute within each hour. At the end of it, his mind was placid, his inner tempo drawn out and stately, his body free of pain. The emblem was adjusted for limited dosing and the presence of the Harbor system reinstituted; that barely perceptible observer lurking in the corner of his brain, listening, waiting, allowing him autonomy until intervention was necessary—that warden, was back.

It crowded him.

The outline of the emblem glowed mostly a faint dark blue, monitoring, inputting nothing, and Kier recognized it as the protocol used for Seda. His surface thoughts were directed to the tasks at hand and his emotions were subdued, but beneath that, he felt surprise at being handled the same way his brother had been, even though it had obviously failed to save him.

Kier mourned for his friend in the lower chambers of his soul, where he had the privacy to think. A dull ache was all he was allowed to feel on the surface.

Patrols were being lengthened in breadth and scope. Kier was walking twice as much each day as he had even a week earlier, and the battles with the Cascade continued unabated. The system had taken to imposing naps on the Sentinels throughout their waking hours, descending on them abruptly regardless of where they were. Resource management required the new regimentation. Without it, they had been advised, the remaining units could not maintain the relentless labor. Patrolling was the only activity that permitted any leeway, giving them time to get to a pod before being shut down.

The morning after that terrible night, the brothers were gathered for the morning meal, and when the names were read, Kier found himself uttering a bitter cry. "Sedakad, my Brother!" escaped his lips before he could think, and it brought to mind former days when other brothers had bemoaned one name above the rest. The memory brought tears, but his eyes would not comply and shed them. Rigidly he was held in the grip of the system.

Underneath, he counted and decided that there were notes to go with those beats. Knowing nothing of music, he still found some that satisfied him. Four notes stepping up on a modal scale, then starting over again. *Re, mi, fa, sol...* there was no talent in it, but it cried out everything that could not be expressed with words.

Once on patrol, Kier marched to the music of the four-note tune that only he could hear. The morning was crisp and clear, filled with a chorus of birds just returning from milder climates they visited in winter, who hadn't lost a brother and didn't know the world had changed. The lawns were green, with a hint of frost. Crocuses were in full bloom, and trees were green tipped with early buds. Everything promised spring, though there were weeks to go of winter, and snow still ruled the skies.

It was a beautiful morning.

Kier examined the neighborhood as he walked, noticing a multitude of contrasts between his life and theirs. They had no vehicles of any kind. He had his own pod and aerial avatar. He never saw them communicating at a distance except through the home system that guarded each house. They had no group coms or digital brain links. They spoke to each other to communicate—like he and Seda had.

They used hand tools for gardening, not equipment, and no one wore armor or carried weapons of any kind. *This is because we are tasked with protecting them*, he reminded himself. They were free to lead a simple, happy life as long as the Sentinels were set apart for defense.

Sleep cycle in five minutes, the system warned. Kier raced back to his pod and settled into his seat just in time. Blackness descended, taking him from full consciousness to dreamless sleep in less than three seconds.

And in those seconds, he saw two Sentinels moving up the street, walking in sync, heading purposefully somewhere.

When Kierkad opened his eyes again the street was empty. Twenty minutes had passed. He pushed himself to move before he was fully awake, flinging the door open, climbing out, steadying himself as a wave of dizziness rocked him. He breathed deeply and shut the pod door. Heading in the direction he had seen the Sentinels go, he propelled his legs at a fast walk, then sped up as he loosened, trotting, leaping, running.

Something was not right. They never went by twos on patrol.

Inside he knew where they had gone. Now that Seda was gone, the impulse of the system was to reassert itself against his influence. And there was one place in Kier's zone, one person, that he was afraid for.

The boy.

Topping the hill and rounding the corner, he saw the boy's home in the distance and the Sentinels arguing in the front yard with a man. *Perhaps he really is the boy's father*, Kier thought as the man turned his head. Caden's face blanched and his eyes widened as he saw Kier barreling down the sidewalk.

"Stop!" Kierkad shouted as his brothers pushed Caden aside. The man threw himself onto one of them to slow him down, but the second Sentinel moved into the house where high-pitched shrieking ensued. In minutes, he reappeared dragging the screaming boy by the arm. By then, Kier had reached them.

"We are retrieving the trespasser," the one holding the boy informed. Kier recognized him as Vadokad. "Do not interfere."

"Over my dead body!" Caden yelled, wrestling with Divadkad, beating him wherever he could land a fist, bloodying his knuckles on the armor which darkened around each blow. Desperation drove him into a frenzy, and he succeeded in knocking the brother over. In a blink, the Sentinel had him flipped onto his back with a hand to his throat, one arm pinned under his knee, and the other pulled out uncomfortably taut with his free hand.

"That is not necessary," Divadkad growled. The system had him restrained, like a dog on a leash, and he didn't harm the father, but Kier knew his brother's eyes would be full of rage, terrifying to look at. He was amazed that Caden stared back and continued to thrash without fear. Or perhaps he was filled with fear, but it looked like wildness, like recklessness.

Kier gripped the upper edge of Divadkad's back-plate and yanked him off the man. "Stand, Sentinel," he ordered. This was his zone and while he patrolled, his authority was solid. It struck him then that the Harbor system had tried to snatch the boy while he was sleeping. This implied deceit. "Release this man," he added.

"Sentinel!" the brother snapped stiffly at attention. His eyes glared at Caden with the ferocity of an animal.

"Sentinel!" Kierkad pointed at the second one and stepped close to him. "Release the boy." The child had stopped screaming and was watching Kier with pleading, tearful eyes, begging him with those eyes to help.

"You are mistaken," Vadokad's voice grated in his throat, as if he were unaccustomed to using it. He leaned in till his face shield had tapped Kier's, eyes to eyes, face to face, rage to rage, though they weren't pressed against each other as the harmonizing would place them. A murderous anger smoldered through the glass. The system restrained him also or there would already have been bloodshed. "You are resisting the Harbor."

"This is my patrol and my zone." Kier stood still meeting his gaze. He wondered if the brother were rehearsing the harmony drill in his mind, hating him, facing his loneliness, tasting despair, groping for love, believing in the farce. Kier no longer did. He just waited and did not back down.

The father rose to his feet and came close to boy, kneeling next to him, wrapping him in an embrace. Gingerly, he began to pry the Sentinel's fingers from his arm, all the time looking at his son. He didn't speak but love flowed from him. All that mattered to him was that boy.

Vadokad let his fingers be loosened one by one and once the boy was free, finally backed down from the face to face confrontation. "I will report back to base without the child," he snarled, his emotions poorly controlled. A sign of breakdown in the system, or perhaps evidence of the recent overuse made of the Sentinels.

"Leave," Kierkad barked, and the two brothers burst out simultaneously with a "Ha!" before running off in synchronized strides, acquiescing, submitting, respecting the Order. Indoctriny guaranteed it.

Kier swiveled and fixed his attention on Caden and his son. *You are in danger*, he wanted to say, *you can't stay here, or they will be back when I am no longer in charge.* But every word he said would be overheard and any warning he gave would be countermanded by the Harbor.

He could not speak as he wished. Maybe, he considered, humans were able to see deeper messages through the link of the eyes.

"Thank you," Caden croaked, his words choked with tears and irritated by the Sentinel's grip on his neck. "My son...my son..." He could get no more out.

CASCADE

"Kierkad," the boy said, surprising both of them, reaching a hand to touch his arm, the same arm where he had planted his fake chip. "You saved me. I knew you would. I knew you were good."

Caden was shaking his head like he wanted to stop him but didn't know how or didn't have any strength left.

"I am noble," Kier responded softly, squatting down next to him and laying his hand over the boy's where it rested on his arm. "It is my calling to protect all of you."

"Some of the others," the boy scrunched his forehead, frowning, "aren't like you. I see them walking around. But you…" He didn't know how to finish.

"I lost my brother last night," Kier whispered to him, and he felt the system's attention grow stronger. He didn't care. Caden looked into his eyes, and compassion replaced some of the torment that had been there. "He was my friend. He is the one who spoke up for you in the Harbor and I honor his words. The Harbor honors his words."

"Him?" the boy gasped. "He was great! Yeah, he said some things and they let me go."

"Yes, they let you go," Kier confirmed. He turned and fixed a stare on the father. He hoped, dared to hope, that the man would understand the warning he wanted to convey. For a long moment, they looked at each other.

"Come, Son," Caden said finally, rising to his feet with the boy's hand in his. "Let's go inside. I'm hungry and you're hungry. And Kierkad needs to patrol."

Kier watched them enter the house. They opened the door, went through, and closed it with a final wave.

The lights inside came on, though there was no need for them, and a radio began to play music, mellow, calming, and peaceful. Curtains rustled where the window had been cracked open and the bare branches of the trees whispered with them.

He saw the stillness resting over the house, but felt the fear simmering under it, and didn't want to leave. Was there a way to stay? Would the Sentinels be sent back when his patrol ended? He had reminded the system of its own choice to honor Seda's words. Would the Harbor respect its own decisions? Did it abide by the Order?

A summons came through as he completed his patrol. He was to meet with Pacificator Nirekad as soon as he returned. Staying behind to guard the boy's house was no longer possible. He may have gained the freedom to nurture his own thoughts and feelings in the under-layer, but it was a far cry from liberty of action. Resisting a direct command was so foreign it hadn't even occurred to him.

The sun was shining as he made his way to the Pacificator's station, a curved windowed room at the end of the training cells. Nirekad stood looking out at the view of the river, hands behind his back, twiddling his thumbs. He wasn't wearing his usual cap and braided gray hair hung down from his balding head leaving visible the emblem of the Order that was lodged there, embedded into the scalp. It glowed with a dark green light.

"You are here, Brother," he greeted Kier without turning around. "I have listened to your interchange with the father and the boy. I have observed it as well."

Kier took a stand a few paces away and spoke. "Yes, Master, I have guarded the boy."

Nirekad spun around and scowled at him. "Your brothers were obeying my command."

Kier wondered at this. What part did Nirekad play in the Harbor system? Did his authority supersede it? "I was obeying my directive as a Sentinel. I have no quarrel with my brothers," was all he said.

"Then you have one with me?" Nirekad challenged, folding his arms across his chest, showing the flab of his arms. He was imposing because the resonance of his voice was commanding and assured, and because he held a high position in the Order, ruling over the brothers in this base. But he looked old and weak, clothed in a rough, brown tunic with a leather belt around his waist and worn leather boots on his feet. Kier remembered some history of the planet and that the model of brotherhood had been copied from their past. This simple garb was familiar to the earthlings as a model of simplicity and purity, meant to convey the idea of monasticism.

"I have no quarrel with you, Master," Kierkad affirmed, cloaking his eyes so that none of his feelings would show. He was guessing at how to do that. It seemed easy since he had used his eyes only for viewing for so long. "I was unaware of your command and the reversal of the system's instruction to overlook the boy's trespass."

"You seem to be unaware of how to respond when a brother tells you they are under orders." He glowered. "You have shown a blatant disregard for me and my authority."

So, he *was* subject to the overarching rule of the Harbor system, and the system hadn't actually reversed the instruction. His maneuvering to snare the boy depended on getting Sentinels to agree with him and act on his behalf. "I honor you, my Brother," Kier stood at attention. "I honor you as our Pacificator."

"You honor the Harbor system..."

"Yes."

"But you seem to be unaware of the measure of respect, the obedience that is appropriate for, your Pacificator. You are lacking a higher...ah...loyalty, I would say." He squinted one eye and cramped his mouth into a twisted knot. "You must learn this if you are to...ah...grow, shall we say."

Kier would trust the Harbor system over Nirekad in any conflicting instructions. His manipulation was pointless, and he was tempted to say so, but he held his peace for several reasons. Nirekad's posture was threatening, and he couldn't tell what to make of it, so he waited to hear more. Second, he didn't like to disobey his superior. And third, he needed to find a way to counter him without compromising his loyalty to the Harbor.

"I am noble," he responded automatically, but was interrupted before he could continue the chant.

"But I wish to speak to you of other things, nobler things..." Nirekad smiled falsely and spread out his hands in a conciliatory fashion. "You are showing great progress in the Order, and we believe you are ready to begin a new level of training."

"Thank you, Brother," he nodded uncertainly, wondering if this would remove him from patrol duty. And who did he mean by 'we'?

"Come," he waved an arm with a grand sweep and ushered Kier toward a table. There was a large map spread out there. "We will begin now."

The map showed land masses and bodies of water. There were many lines, dots, color changes, and notes all over it. Kier understood what it was but didn't know how to interpret it. What region did it represent? And what was the scale? Would he see the Harbor and his own community there?

He found himself leaning over it and studying it hungrily. The greens, browns, and blues beckoned to him like calls from a mythical land. Placing both hands down on the paper with fingers spread, he smoothed it and lowered his head closer. "What is it?" he asked at last with a sigh.

"This," Nirekad nodded smugly, "is our domain. The world of the Sentinels."

"How do I understand it?" Kier countered, reading words, looking for landmarks, scanning the lines and curves—roads, for clues. "Where is the Harbor?"

"I will show you one day," the Pacificator resisted Kier's longing, relishing the hint of power it gave him. "What I want you to understand is how many of us there are." He extended his index finger and drew it across the map in many directions, singling out little dark squares that were sprinkled generously on it. "Here, here, here…" hundreds of them, "These are bases like ours."

Kier gasped. He was impressed. "The Severance is no match for us," he concluded with awe.

"Yes," Nirekad intoned melodically, like he did when he spoke noble words to them. "You need to remember that we are strong, and there is hope. Minor setbacks in small regions are nothing compared to our extensive, powerful, and well-organized Order."

Kierkad was nodding and his heart swelled with pride.

"You are valuable, Brother, your sacrifice of service is noble and precious to the Order."

Kierkad's eyes grew damp, and he blinked several times.

"We continue to protect our flock from the invasion…" Nirekad continued mystically.

"How do they do it?" Kier interjected unable to stop himself, carried away by the emotion the map had stirred. "How do they take our brothers like that?"

A strange light burned in Nirekad's eyes, flickering in marbly white and purple lights, as though something that wasn't in the room reflected in them. For a moment he didn't belong, and he wasn't one of their own, he was an alien thing, ogling and despising him. It lasted merely an instant and was broken and quenched by the fury that followed it. He slammed his hands on the table and a guttural yell burst from his lips.

"Get out!" he bellowed, shattering the noble façade he wore, and Kier hastened to obey, repulsed by the Pacificator's rage and lack of self-control.

One thing was clear. His question had upset the master because he had no answer.

The Cascade was far more sophisticated than he had dreamed.

CHAPTER 9

4 Days

The next day, Kier awoke before dawn to the sound of alarms. Everything within him resisted as he rose to his feet, groggy after only three hours of rest. His legs and arms were leaden, his sight blurry, and confusion hindered him. Moving to his armor, still charging where it hung from the wall, was automatic, but it felt wrong. So wrong. Every Sentinel was prepared to give his life for the noble cause but to be serving day and night without cessation was like being bled dry while still alive.

As he exited into the hall, another Sentinel, one he didn't recognize, entered his room behind him. Kier paused and looked over his shoulder at him, watching as the unknown brother took off his armor, hung it on the wall, and lay down in the bed in the center of the room. He stared at him, unaware for a moment of the wailing signals. The stranger was asleep almost before his arms were crossed over his chest.

The bed was not Kier's own. The room was not set apart for him either. But it was where he had always lived, always slept, always hung his armor. And on the back wall there was a crack where he had hidden a piece of paper in the first days of his life that he could remember. Nothing could have spoken more clearly about his insignificance in the Order than this cursory use of his bed.

He turned and joined the streams of brothers stumbling down the halls away from their rooms as just as many unknown Sentinels thudded the opposite direction to take their places.

Down the passageway he trod, trailing behind the others, barely aware of the sirens, clenching and unclenching his hands to loosen the fingers and waken blood flow. His limbs were sluggish from sleep and his mind numb. Every movement was automatic and mechanical. Snag a couple nutrient packs. Open the door to the pod. Buckle into the seat. Close the door. Flip the switch.

The craft hummed. He ate a few bites and swallowed some fluid. He shook his head and blinked. *Function restored*, he thought as he regained some clarity. Enough at least for the next skirmish.

There were nearly double the number of pods crammed in the hangar. Funneling the Sentinels out the bottleneck of an exit delayed them substantially in getting to their battle posts. The waves of drones that should've taken off nearly simultaneously became a piecemeal trickle, scattering their formations—which were essential in deciphering the Cascade drop patterns. Delays could make fighting in the air futile.

Kier was one of the first out the door but seeing and hearing the difficulty the brothers were facing getting airborne, he found himself acting on an impulse—which wasn't merely unusual, it was completely unknown to him. He *never* acted outside of his mandate. Not consciously. Every small decision he made stayed within an overarching directive to care for the humans.

This is also directed by my care for humans, he rationalized to himself, turning off-path, detouring from the course assigned to him.

Caden's home was a couple streets out of his way, but he had to check on it, and there was time. Coasting down the street, he saw that the houses were all dark as they should be at that early hour, but Caden's front door was open. No one left their house open like that during the night—if they were there.

He stopped the pod and got out, glancing at the emblem on his forearm to confirm that the system hadn't noticed and wouldn't interfere. He had to see inside. The wind had tossed some leaves in the door and the curtains at the window were moving gently, a current of air weaving a path through the house. There was some clutter, scattered around the main rooms, and as he opened each door and looked, the bedrooms showed the same haphazard disarray.

There was no blood. He realized he had been looking for blood. A wave of relief washed over him as he noticed empty drawers and gaping closets, evidence of a hasty departure. The father must have understood. He had gotten away with the boy.

Kier began choking for a moment as he tried to breath and found his throat tightening. It passed quickly leaving a knot he couldn't swallow. *Thank you,* he thought absurdly, groping for a place to direct the thought.

Pain in his arm and urgency from the system kicked in. Kier turned and ran to his pod. The battle was fully engaged now, and he was late. He sped to his station and launched his avatar at breakneck speed, exhilarated by the boy's escape. Taking a steep, accelerating ascent, he curved upward till he was nearly vertical, relishing the gees tugging down on him. A seasoned Sentinel learns to be fully present in their avatar and experience every movement it made as if they were actually flying in their own bodies.

Kier had forgotten what it was like to fly aggressively and reveled in it. Swooping to the right, banking to the left, diving and pulling up, he made up for lost time as he scoured his sector for floats. Normally, he would be starting high in the atmosphere and making a descending sweep, but because of the delay he had decided to start low and head upwards. It was rare for him to take an independent approach in battle, but though the system watched, it didn't resist.

There! A string of floats came into view and cutting through them from underneath, he sliced and burned ten of them before they responded. The Cascade floats had been equipped with tiny jets to help them dodge drones and give them a better chance at reaching the ground, but they only activated when the drones came from above. Kier had taken out nearly a hundred before he had crested the wave. Diving down again meant chasing the few remaining floats to the surface and tracking them down on foot.

There were very few wisps in his sector to contend with, and they were soon extinguished. Holding the last one between his fingers, he thought of the song that haunted his dreams and sighed. Counting to four, he crushed it on the fourth count, smiling faintly. The satisfaction tasted of happiness, but it was too fleeting, and the hollowness it left when it had faded was worse than the depression he had carried since losing Seda.

In the distance, other Sentinels tracked down their prey and he could see the blips of light from their lasers and hear the updates on the coms. They were having a lot of trouble as so many had gotten past their defenses and hit the ground, and there weren't enough Sentinels to cover the territory properly. Kier broke into a trot headed for the nearest group.

Scrrreeeeaach! A roar of voices and noise blasted the audio, distorting it, and he realized something was wrong. But he couldn't figure out which way to go to help.

Jogging in a zigzag across the crest of a hill, expanding his scope of vision, he detected a commotion beyond the park on the west, several miles away. He was awake and loosened up now, so he unleashed his full strength and broke into a run straight for the source of the turmoil. Crackling and static continued to interrupt the Sentinel coms until he was almost there. The words that crystalized were jarring and incomprehensible.

"Stand down! Stand down!" several voices were yelling.

Over them, muffling and confusing their words, the Harbor system was announcing, "Report immediately to Central Plaza for peacekeeping duties. ALL SENTINELS REPORT!" The pressure of urgency pumped through his veins, amplified by the throbbing of the emblem on his forearm, but Kier *knew* the trouble was nowhere in that region. Central Plaza was at the other end of town, and he could see and hear the brothers in conflict directly in front of him, with his own eyes and ears. Their voices had been phased out and were now muted in the audio.

Three Sentinels were battling another Sentinel, taking turns engaging him. When one would step up and begin a memorized fight sequence, the opponent would match his every move with equal skill. For one brief moment, Kier was astonished at the beauty of the sight, at the flashing of dim lights reflected on the armor, at the breathtaking speed and agility of the clash. He had never observed the sequence as a bystander before.

But this was nothing like training. The ferocity was real. The desperation uncontrolled.

And the renegade kept *breaking the pattern*. In the headlong rush of memorized moves, he was interrupting to insert changes, break the flow, and take his opponent off guard. Kier had never witnessed anything like it.

Pow! The Sentinel went flying backward, landing on his back, sliding to a stop, groaning. And another one took his place, throwing himself at the renegade with a loud yell. One after another, the three Sentinels took on their brother and he fought them off, wheeling and thrashing around like a cornered wild animal.

Kier shook himself, realizing he had been staring. "Sentinels!" he bellowed running up to separate them, shoving himself in between them. "Stand down! Stand down!" He remembered he had heard those words on the coms and wondered if he was also being muted. The renegade saw him only as another attacker and leapt at him, pummeling his head with blows. The other brothers stood back to let him fight, and he found himself responding automatically, with increasing aggression as the renegade got through his guard multiple times, landing painful strikes.

It dawned on him that he hadn't actually been fighting. He'd been sparring as if with a friend—and this was not friendly.

The combatant challenged them. "You're all liars!" he yelled. "Get away from me!"

"Sentinel!" Kierkad spat out between blows. "You…are out…of Order…. Stand…down!!"

"NO!" the Sentinel roared in response, all remnants of Order and Indoctriny abandoned. Kier amped up the power in his punches and managed better than the others had. He was more alert to the deviations from the pattern and found them clumsy. The renegade was breaking away from the training in an intentional way but had no skill or wisdom to back it up.

Kier wasn't frantic like the renegade. He was fully alert and focused, battling with all his strength and insight. Dodging the breakout blows became easy as he learned to recognize the 'feint and duck' approach the renegade always initiated with. Before long, he was following them with unpracticed hits of his own. Each one was better timed and stronger than the one before it, until one particularly well anchored wallop, powered through his body with the full force of his legs, knocked the renegade backwards flat. Kier and the other Sentinels were immediately on him, pinning him in the dirt.

He wouldn't submit. He fought and thrashed, gritting his teeth and jerking his head around. "Let me go!" he burst out.

"You are out of Order," one Sentinel rebuked him.

"Anarchy is forbidden," another followed.

"You must return and be reset..." two of them speaking almost in sync began to relay the Harbor's orders.

"What is happening, Brother?" Kier interrupted, pinning his right arm with a knee, leaning on his chest. "Why are you fighting us? What is wrong with you?"

The renegade grew still and latched onto Kier's eyes with a fierce stare.

Those eyes! Kier was shaken by the despair in them. "What is it, Brother?" he spoke more softly now. "Have you lost your center?"

"You..." he grated. "You're looking at me..." meaning more than the words implied.

Kier knew what it was to look at a brother and see a wall. And he knew what it was to see a *person.* "What is your name, Brother?" he asked, wondering if the other Sentinels understood, if they were aware or asleep, if they had walls or windows in their eyes.

"Mev," the renegade said, relaxing his whole body, smoothing the muscles of his face, letting himself sink into the ground and his head drop back on the grass, subdued.

"Mevkad," Kier responded, concerned about the informality. It was dangerous to use shortened names outside the Harbor. "You are upset."

"Yes, I am," he replied, blinking slowly.

"Why? Why are you fighting us?" Kier asked easing back a little on the pressure he had brought to bear on the brother's chest.

CASCADE

"I can't bear it anymore," he whispered, shaking his head, rolling it gently sideways, back and forth where it lay in the grass. "The game…it's hopeless…. It's all hopeless…"

"What game?" Kier countered evenly.

"All of this," Mevkad said, swallowing. "The Cascade, the Harbor, the Order…. It's nothing but a farce. We're all lost, and this is the abyss. This is our punishment…our prison…to fight empty shadows forever…"

"The people we are defending are real," Kier affirmed, but he was uneasy inside. Was Mevkad really saying out loud the thoughts that sometimes tormented Kier in the night?

"The people are real, but what do they care if the floats fall?"

"We are preventing the return of the Severance," the Sentinel holding his left arm replied, sounding confident.

"We're the only ones who are ever hurt by the Cascade. We're the ones *dying* every day. And no one cares. All those people we came to protect, that we gave up *everything* to serve…" Mevkad closed his eyes, and his words seemed to come from deep inside, intoned with groans of despair. "What do they care if one of us is gone? Another will take our place." He gasped for air, taking several deep, heavy breaths.

"The Noble Call…" the Sentinel pinning Mevkad's feet began, his voice portraying the assurance Kier had enjoyed all his life until recent days. The contrast between then and now pierced him with melancholy.

"I thought it was noble," Mevkad said, lifting his head to look at the one who had spoken. "But it's all lies. I never volunteered for this. I never wanted to be so alone…so destitute…my life has no meaning, Brother."

Kier leaned back farther, still holding onto Mevkad's arm. The others followed suit and the renegade brother sat up. The system began to appeal to them to return to the Harbor and bring the captive to Restoration. They all felt it. But none of them moved. Kierkad had taken down the rebel, so they watched him and waited to follow his lead. And he wasn't ready to go yet.

"Life has meaning," Kier countered, groping within himself for some truth to back that up. He thought of Caden. *Seda helped the boy escape the first time, and I, the second,* he thought. "Our lives have a purpose."

"Yes," one of the other brothers nodded, with a hint of relief.

"Have you seen the chips?" Mevkad glared at Kier. "They crush to dust in our fingers like chalk, like mere clumps of sand."

"We are strong," someone said.

"And those flashes of data," Mevkad went on, letting his gaze rest on one and then another, searching for support or understanding. "They zap at us with nonsense and sometimes pictures. What residue does that leave? How is that causing damage? What do we care if a thousand of them accumulate on the ground?"

A stunned silence hung around them. The Harbor listened and decided to intervene.

"If they are harmless then who is wiping out the Sentinels?" one of the brothers who hadn't spoken yet became the Harbor's voice. It gave Kier a hint of satisfaction to recognize the influence. He used to think that they were all conduits of the Harbor's voice, working in sync, but now he knew that the Harbor looked for Sentinels to speak through because it wouldn't, or perhaps couldn't, force them.

"The Severance is taking us out so it can return..." one of the others answered.

Mevkad laughed bitterly. "I used to believe that!"

The brother at his left arm turned to look at Kier with fear in his eyes, floundering, finding the teachings of Indoctriny shifting under his feet.

Kier had no reassurance for him.

"Why have you rejected it now?" Kier asked, remembering how Seda had vanished from within the room before he could bust the door open. He was sure that only the Severance could have done that.

"You have been tampered with," the Harbor said, speaking through the cooperative Sentinel. "The data streamed at you from those chips has coalesced into a false configuration of reality. If we do not defend the people, which is our vow and our calling, they will be helpless when the invasion returns. We must not abandon our post."

The words were stirring, and the system enforced it with some euphoric dosing to increase their reaction. Kier felt the boost in a superficial way, but his under-layer was untouched, and the fissure between the two parts of himself widened.

It affected Mevkad differently as well, distressing him. He hung his head as if to weep—but Sentinels have no tears. Sorrow had no outlet and built within them like an abscess.

"I wish that were true..." Mevkad moaned. "I fight day and night with all my strength, joining all of you, to make it true. But there's nothing underneath except emptiness and I can't sustain myself with lies anymore."

"Brother!" the one on Mevkad's left begged, "Let us take you back. You will be restored!"

"I can't stop you," he whispered. "But it won't help."

"You belong there, with us," the brother continued.

"No!" Mevkad's eyes darted around, "I don't belong there! And no one cares. When I am lost…" He began fumbling for words as if his tongue had grown thick. "There are others…lots of others…no room for me…" His head dropped forward onto Kier's shoulder as he passed out, the emblem on his chest-plate throbbing green and blue. The system was done waiting and wasn't going to permit another attempt at escape.

And where could he run?

Kier glanced around. No humans were in the streets and no lights in the windows. Odd. Wouldn't the yelling and fighting have brought at least a few to observe?

Kier wrapped his arms around Mevkad and rose to a stand with the others' help, bracing him against his shoulder. The Sentinel who had spoken for the Harbor sent one of the others to get Mevkad's pod and while they waited no one made a sound.

It bothered Kier that he didn't know their names. He used to know all his brothers. But now that turnover had become so high, and almost double the complement overflowed the Harbor, he had stopped trying to learn them.

"I miss the Canyon Base," the brother who had been afraid confessed.

Kier was shocked. "Did you come from another base?" he asked. He had never considered the *reason* for the influx of brothers to the Harbor, and it bothered him that the question hadn't even occurred to him.

"Yes," he answered. "There weren't many of us left. Just new recruits, untrained. And that didn't…uh…well, it was good they transferred us here. You, here at the Harbor, are the best and we have a lot to learn."

"How many of you?" Kier felt the system press on him to stop talking but he resisted.

"Twenty-thhh…um…" The brother's voice faded out and he stood staring at the ground.

"And other bases retreated to our base, too, didn't they?" Kier got the question out into the open before the system could stop it, in spite of the pressure building on his arm. He had taken the new Sentinels for granted, believing them to be reinforcements and an expansion of power on Earth. He had told himself they would build more bases to house them which was both intimidating and impressive. But it was a lie. The Order was dwindling, and the remnants were being collected as they retreated.

"Our base leads the Order in skill and success," the Harbor guided Sentinel said. "It is a privilege for others to come and learn our tactics and fight with us. There's no reason to be alarmed about the numbers."

Mevkad's pod arrived. The brother driving it got out and helped to put the sedated Mevkad in. The Harbor took over from there, engaging a homing sequence and sending the pod on its way. The other Sentinels trotted off, each toward his own pod.

Kier hesitated.

Sentinels were trained to observe, not detect when they were the ones being observed. The feeling he had, that someone lurked in the shadows watching him, was out of character and a little unnerving. He rotated around carefully, searching with infrared, scanning trees, bushes, windows, doors, and shadows. Nothing obvious.

Unsatisfied, he searched again, only this time, he let himself be guided by instinct. Where did he *feel* like someone was hiding? The house with the blue shutters. He walked toward it and the sense of being watched increased. There was a darkened window that didn't have the curtains drawn and he imagined someone hiding in there, behind furniture, peering around at him.

He drew closer to the window, knowing he would be able to see inside once he was close enough, but the notion of a person pulling away, filled with anxiety, gave him pause. Whoever was in there was afraid, and he didn't *want* to frighten them.

Backing away, he turned and started the long walk to his pod, thinking about what had been said.

No one had ever voiced so many doubts in his hearing before and he wondered how Mevkad had succeeded. The Harbor usually suppressed them. Hearing them stated openly, discussed in the hearing of several brothers, was troubling.

Why are we resisting the Cascade? he asked himself intentionally for the first time. Talking with Mevkad had magnified his sense of dislocation. The Order had always been a shelter for him, an identity, a place to belong. Now, his inner self had fallen out of that refuge and hung from a thread over nothing.

The Noble Call no longer guarded Kier's soul.

CHAPTER 10

2 Days

Conquest Timeline:
Twenty years to spread deception
Five years to provoke unrest
Six months to train the troops
Seven days for invasion
—Severance communique to the Jagged Edge
strategist

The sun was shining brightly in the morning, as if spring had already come, and Kier's patrol was quiet and soothing. He smiled as he walked, enjoying the human activity that greeted days like this one. People walking to work, children's voices, birds and dogs, squirrels and rabbits. Sometimes they waved at him, and he waved back. The hum he intoned was the one he saved for his best days. It merely kept one note for a long time, then stepped up a note, then down a couple notes, then returned to the first note. The vibration in his throat was comforting.

Rounding the corner of Caden's street, he saw new people coming out the door, as if they had always lived there. Hugs and kisses, goodbye calls, footsteps walking away, nodding in his direction. He paused at the path in front of it and stared at it.

The system noticed. It scanned his memory records and tested his status.

Kier hummed and moved on.

I am not supposed to remember, he thought in the under-layer. The Harbor combed through the Sentinels' memories and often chose some to extract and archive, and they were accustomed to it. But Kier had discovered that he had a second reservoir of thought and memory that the Harbor couldn't access, and that was where he had stored the ones he wanted to keep.

The child's crayon drawing was there.

Kier called up data on the family that had taken Caden's residence. It struck him that the records never explained how long someone had lived somewhere, or how long they had worked at a particular job.

Time references were irrelevant to a Sentinel.

By design.

"Excuse me, Sentinel," a woman's voice broke into his thoughts. "I was wondering if you could help me." She was tall and thin, with limp, straight brown hair and dark brown eyes. She wore dark blue, office-work garb, and a black winter coat. He had scanned and identified her before her words had been completed.

"I am here for you," he responded. This answer connected to both layers within him. As a Sentinel he was invested in his role, and as an individual, somewhere in secret, he cared about the flock.

"We've been here for three weeks and our connection to the mainframe is still not working." She creased her brow and pressed her lips together, pointing over her shoulder at the house with a tricycle in the yard. "I know it's a privilege to get into the Valley of Gentle Hearts and I am grateful, but my work depends on being able to access other regions in a timely way. I can't get my…"

"Other regions…" Kier echoed while he thought about her words. He had been on missions to areas nearby before, and the concept was familiar. But he found her words confusing and illogical. People lived in houses and walked to work in town, over the hill. Then they came home. What was taking place inside the home? What did she mean?

"Yes," she huffed, crossing her arms. "You're obviously well equipped for any issue. Can't you come look at it?"

"In your house?" He considered it, calling to mind the floor plan and all the blueprints showing plumbing, electricity, and other systems. He could see that they were working well without entering the home. "Of course, I will if you wish. Perhaps you have forgotten the instructions…"

"Not likely," she muttered under her breath as she turned to lead him in. The living room was cluttered with stacks of books and papers, shoes in a tumble near the door, coats strewn over the couch, and scattered toys suitable for children of single digit ages. The kitchen had stacks of dishes in the sink. As far as he knew, the mainframe was not required for maintaining order of this kind.

"Your home is messy," he observed and was surprised by her reaction.

"What do you expect when we're not allowed robots? Not even the most basic cleaners!" The redness of her skin and the twisting of her features clearly spoke of anger, an illogical response. The system quickly fed him the tool he needed.

"I am sorry I offended you," he said. "It was not my intent. I know nothing of maintaining a home."

"I know! I know," she snapped. "Look, over here…" With a wave, she brought up the dark warm holo that served as the interface to the mainframe. It shimmered in a flat rectangle over the wall at eye level. "I can get to here, this camp…" She pulled the image of the camp toward the room, expanding it, and it opened into a standard entry. "Then right here, it stops. I'm blocked." The entry panel featured numerous options, but the main door refused to open. No reason was given.

Kier placed his right hand on the holographic interface and the emblem on his chest-plate lit up. He had expected immediate access, but he was also denied. He attempted various work arounds, tools he had used easily before, and nothing worked.

"Access is denied," he informed the woman. He turned to look at her and she was gazing right at him, into his eyes.

"I know," she said, staring, "That's why I asked for help."

"I am not able to help you." He dropped his hand and turned to face her.

"Thank you for trying," she whispered, searching his face. She looked as if she had forgotten something and was trying to find the memory in him. "I'm going to have a hard time keeping up with my responsibilities in other regions…. The time zones are different, and I'm not allowed to be in the office at any times other than the standard shift."

Time zones. Kier stared at her. What did that remind him of?

"I really love my work…" she turned back to the holo interface and attempted entry again. "I don't understand what the delay is…"

He knew she was a teacher, working long distance with isolated communities, including a handful in distant bases in the solar system. Her work was funneled through a station in a different region. With a different time zone. "I'm sorry I haven't been able to solve your problem."

"Will you stop by tomorrow?" She whipped around and glared at him. "You're the closest thing I've found to someone in charge, and I know that eventually, someone will listen if I just keep asking, even if I'm asking the wrong person."

"My patrol leads me this way every day." *Why would time change in different places?* was the question that had his attention. He almost voiced it aloud but that would be unwise.

"I'll take that as a yes," she strode to the front door, opened it, and stepped aside, a clear invitation to leave.

Kierkad exited. "Day," he commented over his shoulder.

"New day," she called as she closed the door, pushing a gust of air after him.

Kier searched the data on her again but didn't find where she had come from.

He knew the Earth was round. He knew the sun was the center of the Solar System and he was familiar with the outposts on other planets and their moons, orbiting stations, satellites, and transport grids in space. But he didn't understand how the regions fit onto the planet—*or how time was bent by it.*

It was an incongruent and discordant idea, but he couldn't let it go. There was some core of truth in it he wanted to strain out. Time. The regions of time. The zones of time.

It meant something.

Wrapping up the patrol with a quickened step and head held high, Kier felt happier, on both layers, than he had in some time.

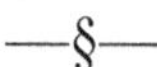

"Kierkad," Pacificator Nirekad intoned melodically, as though he were bringing him into a new realm of privilege with that one utterance of his name. He accompanied the greeting with a wide sweep of his arm, ushering him into the office he had visited a few days before, where he had seen the map.

"Master," Kier responded with a gentle bow as he entered. The table at the side still had the unrolled map, its corners weighted with stones. He glanced at it longingly, pining for the knowledge it held.

"Come and sit." Nirekad settled himself in his chair near the fire and gestured toward another chair pulled up at the other corner of the hearth, ready for a guest. A small table held trays of food and mugs of tea.

Kier approached and hesitated. He stared at the composition before him, with chairs and fireplace, food and drink. A place for his leader and an empty place for… who was that for?

"Be seated," Nirekad reiterated, pointing to the chair. "I wish to speak with you in comfort and since I no longer have… since I have been upgraded to a rank that requires skills unlike any you would need, for diplomacy and…uh…negotiation these arrangements are more suited to my role. And they've become part of my joy."

Kier sat in the chair without resting his back against it. He looked into the fire, glanced at the food and drink, took in the view through the window of the river bound by snow, dusk shrouding the trees and water so that the snow glowed in the moonlight.

He saw the beauty and felt the warmth, he smelled the aromas, and his chest ached with a memory he couldn't retrieve. When had he seen such things? When had he known of two chairs at a fire before?

"Eat," Nirekad commanded as he began to take morsels in his fingers from the tray next to him and put them in his mouth.

Kier imitated him, picking up bite-sized pieces and putting them into his mouth, chewing and swallowing. When Nirekad drank, he drank also.

"Aren't you hungry?" Nirekad laughed. "You don't have to keep pace with me. I know a Sentinel's capacity for food. You have a full tray, and you may empty it while I talk."

Kier sped up his consumption, eating at a more normal pace. He hardly thought about the taste or satisfaction unique food like this should give him; he merely recognized that it was special. He was too tense to let himself enjoy it.

"Good food is wasted on the brothers," Nirekad sighed, shaking his head. He was clearly enjoying every mouthful, slurping, 'hmm'ing, making various noises of appreciation, and gulping the tea.

He had said he would talk while Kier ate, but Kier's food was eaten long before the Master was done. Contemplating the fire, the darkening window, and the small touches of comfort in the room kept his attention as he waited. It relaxed him in spite of himself.

"Kierkad," Nirekad said finally, after the last swallow and a dab of cloth on his face and fingers. "I am aware of your growth as a Sentinel. Your independent thought."

The words shocked him like lightning, pressing his chest with heaviness and tightening his throat. He barely breathed as the next few moments passed, and the Master went on.

"It's unusual for a Sentinel to retain the honor and skill he has and to also build a platform… I like that word, platform. It gives a distinct impression of something… something higher, because that's what it is, Brother. It's a higher stratum. You've attained something few have." He leaned back and folded his hands across his belly, a particularly round one at the moment, and punctuated his conversation with burps and deep breaths, the lids dropping over his eyes drowsily. "I have, of course. I'm a Master. I have been one for a long, long time."

Nirekad darted a piercing glance at Kier and resumed. "I'm allowed to consider *Time*."

He let that sink in. Kier gazed into the fire and let his astonishment surface. He forgot that the system, perhaps Nirekad himself, watched his thoughts and feelings. The Harbor let him have his reverie. It gave him room to ponder and wish—long for.

Nirekad watched him now, a smug, knowing look on his face.

All his questions about time, everything he longed to know about how long things had been happening or when they happened or how events happen with a sense of time, all surged within him.

"Ah," the nearly inaudible sound burst from his lips. He could not prevent it.

"Life takes place in an orderly fashion governed by *Time*, Kierkad," Nirekad pressed, drawing him in. "You must have sensed this…"

"Yes." Softly the word escaped as he gazed into the fire.

"And you must have questions…" Nirekad paused but this time Kier was silent. "Sentinels are not called to function on a timeline, but to exist in the present. But some… a few… evolve beyond their station…"

Kier's heart was pounding. The words were intoxicating. A door was swinging open. A door into larger realms, wider expanses, where he could ask and find answers, explore and learn, grow and change… He moaned and covered his face with his hands.

"You are one of these, Kierkad." Nirekad whispered.

"How do you know?" he snapped back, clutching at the Master with a desperate stare, that hungry gaze that demands to be fed, his hands gripping the sides of the chair.

"I see," he said calmly. "I see the deeper *you*."

Terror arced through Kier's body jolting him out of his seat. He found himself standing at attention, waiting. For execution or expulsion from the Order. Or something equally dreadful.

Nirekad made no effort to relieve him though he knew well the state he was in. "A dangerous course lies ahead of you, Brother," he said, rising to his feet and leaning close into his face. "I will lead you along the edge of the precipice. And you may survive, like I have. You may find the strength to attain the next level with me."

Kier focused his gaze on Nirekad and read his face. There were layers of shadow. His eyes sparkled with intelligence and cunning, and though he read respect in them, he also saw mockery. He sensed the snare laid out, the bait on the hook. He felt the poverty of the master's offer, but his need was so great he could not refuse.

The need to be known, to walk together with someone, was deeper than the need for life itself.

"I see you are willing," Nirekad said with a slit of a grin. "Tomorrow. Come here after the morning meal. Your patrol has been reassigned."

"Master," Kier acknowledged and retreated. The force of the command to depart was powerful in his weakened state. He no longer doubted that Nirekad ruled the Harbor and made use of the system whenever he wished.

He had seen the thought in his eyes and then the Harbor had compelled him to obey.

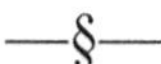

The images in sleep were turbulent and full of confusion. Kier revisited a number of the events of that day, oscillating from sitting at the fire in Nirekad's office, to walking his patrol enjoying the sunshine, to placing his hand on the holo interface in the woman's house. *There is no order to them,* a voice narrated as if it were his own mind, *they are equally accessible to me, whenever I wish.*

He wanted to place them in order. As he tried to make sense of the timing, more events came to mind jumbling up the sequence. The first meal of the day and the last, sparring with Seda, fighting with Mevkad.

Flying in the drone and running on the ground to locate wisps. *It is good*, the words advised. *I am well.*

But he wasn't well. He didn't believe it.

The memories kept replaying. One of the times when he found himself back in the woman's house, he saw a small box sitting on a counter, shaped like a cube with a golden lid etched in glittering light. He hadn't noticed it before. It was quite beautiful. Then, when he revisited the master's hearth, he noticed it on the floor, reflecting firelight with a golden sheen. After that, he noticed it in every memory his mind brought up.

He began searching for the box in each one and soon, wrestling with time and sequence lost its significance. He would just sit down in each memory and close his eyes as though he wanted to stop thinking. Suddenly, a heavy burden lifted off of him and with a big sigh he fell backwards. He remembered that he was lying in bed with his arms crossed and he was alone, but the thought had become comforting.

Now I can look for that box, he thought, and his memories became new images, taking him into realms he had never known, through mountains and valleys, houses and ships, along roads and paths, riding horses, swimming lakes and walking. He never got tired or thirsty. He was never lost. The search for the box gave meaning to his roamings and as he traveled, he would introduce himself as the Brother Who Had a Box and rumors about him spread before him. Soon every land greeted him with news and legends about the box, and he would share what he had heard in other realms.

The journey was an exquisite joy.

When he began to swim up from the depths of slumber, before the surface had fully parted, he glanced down at his hand and saw the box there, glistening with the light that shimmered down from wakefulness. He stared at it and longed for it. He wished to bring his other hand around to open it but couldn't make it move. And as he woke, he traced the artful carving on the gilded lid with his eyes, tasting the memory, smelling it, groping to drop back into the sleep that held it. But he could not.

The call had sounded, and the Sentinels were awake. Kier sat up with his arms still crossed and clung to the picture of the box in his mind. The design was familiar.

It was the childish pencil etching of the boy's chip.

CHAPTER 11

30 hours

I thought I had a home, but I did not
I thought you were my friend, but you were not
I thought my life would count, but it has not.
—Laments of the Severance, cant 34

Kierkad slammed himself into his armor against the wall and raced down the passageway in a stream of brothers, all humming in low harmonious tones, syncing minds and hearts before they reached the hangar.

Cascade.

The Harbor was waking the Sentinels in waves, improving on the disorder of the day before. One after another, they leapt into their pods, revved up and sped out, pouring from the exit in droves. The battle was already underway, and the reports were coming in thick and fast. "Float stream across the river, need support… floats overhead… searching…" Sometimes a brother's cry as he flamed a float came through. Mostly, there were pleas for backup or coordinates for new swarms. Some of them were powered floats that scattered when discovered, some fell helplessly in the air currents.

Racing to his station, not far from his normal patrol grounds, Kier let the residue of his dream empower his excitement for the battle. Soaring into the sky in the avatar, sweeping in wide curves to the left and to the right, for the sheer joy of flying, he waltzed his way into the chaos. At the screams and shouts of brothers colliding—there were too many in close quarters—he was unconcerned. It was a part of being a Sentinel, part of the Noble Call.

"Aha!" he cried out as he zeroed in on a cluster of floats, wheeling around them in a tightening spiral. He had imagined this, plotting in the drowsy moments before falling asleep, how he would whip them into a current they couldn't escape and tighten the noose. He laughed as he flamed one after another.

A chip brushed against the visuals, spitting its code, grating on him. After that, many more tapped into the drone as he cut through them with the wings, sticking for an instant, blurting out streams of data, binary messages, constantly repeated. The downloads began trickling into his buffers where his normal mind automatically attempted to decode and catalogue them.

Gibberish. Kier leaned into the gees as he accelerated and tightened the spiral around the floats. *Strrrzzz! Crytsssss! Frrrrnnggg!* They sparked and flashed and dinged his wings as he cut them down.

Incomplete string. Kier powered on, deciding he wouldn't announce his progress into the

Sentinel audio. It was too cluttered by voices with more urgent calls.

Indecipherable. The cluster was cleared but there were hordes overhead and some beneath him, nearing the ground. He hesitated merely an instant and chose down.

A deep dive fit his mood, plummeting faster than gravity would've pulled him. Speeding past the floats he wondered breathlessly if he could survive a crash, if he would self-destruct before hitting the ground and lose his consciousness in the explosion, or if he would come to himself.

Pull up. The system began to pressure him, and he was unable to resist what both the suppression and his own mind knew to be necessary. He pulled up out of the dive, hooking into another spiral, this time going up and curving the opposite direction. He managed to slice another twenty or so floats before they touched down and it was time to pursue on foot.

Disengaging from the drone, he sunk back into his own frame where discipline awaited him. The Harbor had been pumping him with fear hormones and a few moments after he had experienced the full assault, immediately countered it, adding numbing, subduing chems to regulate it. It was a sickening, gut-wrenching slam that left him trembling as he climbed out of the pod. Worse than blows. Worse than being knocked out.

He took a few shuffling steps in the direction of the fallen wisps, breathing deeply, willing himself to calm down, fighting against nausea. The worst of it passed as he moved down the block. He made his way along the street, slower than his normal pace, and let his thoughts wander as he searched for wisps. Flaming them with his laser was such a mindless task that he barely noticed what he was doing. He saw the crumpled cloths and zapped them and moved on.

In the drone, it wasn't possible to access his inner thoughts, but once he re-centered himself in his body, he regained the connection. The memory of his dream and the gibberish code were waiting for him.

Flickers of his dream returned to his mind, and he recalled the box. He imagined himself opening the box and peering into it, gazing deeply into it, diving in and swimming down with his thoughts, looking for something, seeking the puzzle or the key to the puzzle. The farther he delved, the thicker it became, murky and viscous, dark and claustrophobic, but he pressed on and broke through the blockade. Beyond it, swimming up from the depths, through lighter and calmer realms, he resurfaced into awareness.

He was standing stock still in front of what had been Caden's house, looking down at his empty hand where he had imagined the box to be. He felt no suppression and no rebukes of Indoctriny harnessing him. The waves of queasiness were gone.

The home had lights on. He had known it would. The door was closed, as he had imagined it. There was a room inside that he knew was not empty. He could see it clearly in his mind, the walls, the bed and dresser, the windows and closet doors. He could see pictures on the wall and toys on the floor.

"Sentinel!" a voice yelled from somewhere in the distance accompanied by the pounding of running feet. "Cease!"

He cared little for the drama playing out behind him. Let other brothers respond. Kier would open the door to that room and find what must be there. He strode to the front of the house and knocked. "Sentinel search," he announced as he opened the door. Even if it had been locked, the door would not have resisted him. All entrances were encoded to permit entry to the Sentinels.

A woman shrieked as he opened the door and stepped over the threshold. A man jumped in front of him and began jabbering, asking him what the trouble was, offering to help, pleading with him to stop. Kier shoved him aside firmly, without excess force, and stepped past him. Down the hall, doors popped open, and children stuck their heads out.

"Don't resist him!" the mother screamed down the hallway. More yells from all the family members were tossed around him as he took a few measured paces and stopped, right at the door he wished to enter. The child who had been in there had run out as he drew near and hid in another room.

He placed his hand on the door and turned the knob. The people behind him grew still as they watched.

The window was open, and the curtains fluttered in the cold wind. It wasn't quite right, not like he had pictured. The bed faced a different direction and there was nothing dropped on the floor. No crayons or paper anywhere.

"We tried to redirect him," he heard an anxious voice whisper from the front of the house, "but he's fixed on this house…"

I am fixed on this house, he thought. He didn't want to leave.

"Stand down!" he heard a brother order as human cries picked up again.

"No! No! Wait!" an unknown voice was belting out, getting closer. He turned in time to see a man backing into the room Kier was in followed by two Sentinels, glowing darkly in the armor of anger.

"You are a subversive," one of them accused, pointing at the man.

Before his eyes, the shape of the man changed and twisted, growing larger, thinner, and darker. His eyes glowed and his teeth grew pointed and long, sticking out of his lips. He snarled and spat and laughed at them, mocking. He pulled a long sword from a sheathe behind his back and began swinging it around.

The Sentinels were cautious, holding out their hands to ward off the swings, but not pulling their weapons, circling him cautiously, constrained by the small room. The unhuman beast blasted them with unearthly yells and barked orders at them, commanding them to leave.

"You have unleashed a terrible plague on the Earth," one of the Sentinels said, his armor growing still darker. A long slim metallic wing with a jagged edge unfurled from his forearm, extending toward the man.

Kierkad gawked as the Sentinel unveiled its darker side and found himself unnaturally provoked by it. Anger flowed through him, and he turned to the beast, the *subversive* that the Cascade had planted. He gestured at the thing with his own arm, also growing dark.

"You have been exposed for what you really are!" Kierkad snapped, stepping closer, pressing the creature against the brother with the jagged edge. "You will be brought to justice for your sabotage."

A string of gibberish, worse than all the chips he had ever seen, strung together in a massive blast of data, poured from the vile thing's mouth in squeaks and cries, as he raised his sword and dove at Kierkad, swinging it with all his might. With one powerful move, Kierkad stepped toward him, ducking under the blow, blocking it with his arm-plate and twisting to knock the subversive off balance. It crashed to the floor.

The stream of sounds from his crooked lips died down to a whisper and fizzled out.

"Well done, Brother," the Sentinel who had chased the enemy into the room said. His armor was lightening, and the metallic wing had vanished. He gripped Kierkad's shoulder and yanked him toward the door, propelling him into the hallway, through the house, and out the front door.

"Report to Restoration immediately and then to Pacificator Nirekad," he ordered with the full authority of the Harbor.

Kierkad ran to obey.

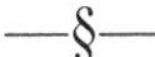

Restoration did not allow him to sleep. He was encased in the shell and hooked up to the stabilizers, but the entire time it was treating him, the system was exploring his mind, cross-examining, searching, testing, demanding answers for everything he had done since the latest battle began. It challenged his reckless behavior in the nosedive he had taken and reprimanded him for entering the house alone. The house itself, he was informed, had harbored a fugitive that had been wanted for questioning who had turned out to actually be a subversive agent. In this, Kierkad's instincts had been accurate. But he was seriously out of Order.

Kier was expelled from the restoration unit before the system had even finished asking questions and sent directly to the Pacificator's chambers without detouring for a meal like everyone else. His body complained at the hunger and the weariness. His mind rebelled at the coercion and rebuke, but he felt no remorse over his behavior or concern over the system's disapproval. He knew he had fought more effectively than the others, and his independent thinking was the reason. He didn't need to explain that.

Nirekad was at the table with the map when he arrived and without looking around at him, waved Kier over to join him.

Kier approached, hunger and weariness forgotten, and fastened his eyes onto it. *Where are we?* he wondered.

"Here," Nirekad said, pointing to a black spot in one of the green portions of the map, chilling him to the bones. *He clearly could read his mind!* "Yes, I can," he added, tapping the emblem on the top of his head, pulsing green and blue. It was uncovered, like it had been the previous time Kierkad had been invited into this chamber.

"Are you the system?" Kier asked. He had intended to ask if Nirekad controlled the Harbor system, but these words came out faster.

"You could say that," Nirekad replied, rotating his head to look at him. His eyelids were narrowed as he stared at Kierkad.

Kier sensed and was surprised by the distrust. "Was it you questioning me in Restoration?"

"Some of it," was the reply. Nirekad turned back to the map and began pointing. "These bases here have been evacuated. This one is in danger. Over here," he stretched his arm and leaned across the map to reach. "These bases are holding. But we still have a swathe of unguarded territory all through here…" He swept along the patch with an open hand.

Nirekad faced Kierkad, crossing his arms over his chest. "What you did today was very important,

Kierkad." His voice belied the praise, projecting frustration instead of satisfaction. "We are hard pressed and the reason for our losses is clear."

Kierkad tore his gaze away from the map to look at the master.

Nirekad searched his mind, staring at him, groping around as if with clumsy fingers in the dark. Kier decided to offer him a thought and presented the memory of the spiral when he had trapped a whole cluster of floats by himself. *Tactics*, he thought.

"Tactics *are* one of our problems..." Nirekad took the offering. "But it won't be enough. No matter how many times we improve our tactics against the Cascade, they adapt and find new ways to challenge us. They hide among the flock, masquerading as innocent people. And one by one they are wiping out the brothers. We are *already* at a point where alien forces could conceivably invade the earth again and gain a foothold."

He leaned toward Kierkad, eyes bulging with widened lids. "And we would not be able to stop them!"

"Alien invasion..." Kierkad tested those words aloud, wondering what it would look like. *Agents*, the thought came to him, *sent ahead to cause dissension and weaken the defenses*. Kier accepted it from the master's mind and puzzled over it. How would they do that?

Nirekad waited and watched his face.

"The creature I saw was a subversive agent from an alien force..." Kierkad suggested, "Is that what you're saying? He's been working in the shadows to weaken our defenses. How would he do that?"

The smug look he had seen on Nirekad's face once before returned. Kier's inner self noticed the hint of disdain but avoided focusing on it while the master's full attention was on him. On the surface, he returned to the lesson he was being taught.

"Are they directing the Cascade somehow?" he caught the approval Nirekad wanted him to see and ignored the gloating he detected underneath.

"It's a terrible thought, isn't it?" Nirekad raised an eyebrow. "If only we knew how it was done."

"Or how it has managed to wipe out so many brothers," Kierkad added, turning back to study the map. He felt a brief surge of disgust from the Master that spilled over just before Nirekad retreated from his link into Kierkad's mind. It was a relief to be free of him and Kier found it hard to repress the urge to take a deep breath.

The map held many regions unknown to Kier apparently without Sentinel bases. They were nestled in distant valleys, on mountain ranges, along coastal plains, in forests, by lakes. He wondered if there were wild animals or perhaps ruins of the old civilizations from long ago. There were myriad lines of crisscrossing roads, some of which he recognized, that spread over the whole thing, except for the water.

He had never seen such expanses of water. "What are those stretches there?" he asked, pointing to vast blue patches. "Is it water like these little pieces here where we are?"

"Ocean," Nirekad grumbled. He had sunk into his own thoughts and was staring into the corner of the room.

There were circles for the communities around the Harbor that Kierkad and the brothers patrolled and protected. Other circles were scattered around other places all over the map. A wild and desperate thought pierced him. *Inhabited places, far from the Harbor!*

Were there places where people lived without the Sentinels?! It was both a frightening thought and an exhilarating one.

"Has the enemy already landed?" he asked. "Are these other regions under alien control?"

Nirekad narrowed his eyes and glared at him, studying his face without invading his mind again. "What is this?" was all he said.

Kier pointed at areas with communities but no Sentinel bases. "Has the Severance returned?"

"Kierkad," Nirekad said purposefully. "There must be no more delay. You are ready for more and I need your help."

Kier stared at him, straightening his body, not at attention, but ready for action. "Master."

"Come with me." Striding to the back of the room beyond the map table, a portion of the wall slid away revealing a long dark hallway. Nirekad strode down it purposefully. The wall glided shut behind them as soon as Kier had entered. Turning sharply to the left, the hall led them into a room with six well-cushioned chairs spaced out around a half-height dome-topped column in the center. He placed both hands on the top of the dome and it hummed as it warmed to life, and subtle light begun to glow deep within it; shimmery greens and blues like the master's emblem colors, and white sparks flashing arbitrarily. Then warm gold and red swirls arose, blending with them, accompanied by deeper humming, the same note an octave lower.

"Sit down and strap in," he ordered as he chose a chair and did the same.

Kierkad obeyed, sitting in the seat closest to him and strapping in.

"Rest your head in socket and let it connect. Don't fight it!" Nirekad commanded as he shoved his head into place and his eyes rolled back in his head.

Kier felt a pang of anxiety as he pressed his head back into the socket and felt it grip him, locking him rigidly into place, and immediately plugging into his access ports. That was what the restorators did on a regular basis, but this was very different. It took complete control of him.

What was it? He couldn't even express a clear thought. Only in his innermost self was he able to form the question. It was another system—a much stronger one. Yanking him from his body, it pulled and pulled, drawing him farther and farther till he felt strained to the limit of tolerance and terrified that the thread that linked him to his own frame would snap. He was helpless against the dread. And the thing that dragged him grew in size, filling the space all around him as if he had been swallowed alive and would suffocate. He wanted to thrash and couldn't. He fought to breathe but there were no lungs to fill.

It was a darkness unlike night, unlike space, unlike depression. A consuming waste that sucked on his life force as if he were food, absorbing whatever was unique in him, whatever was pleasant, whatever he loved.

Shifting in a slow swirling motion, the force that tugged began to thrust him into another frame, shoving him into a clunky, cold, hardened shell fit for lesser beings, not him. Crookedly, heartlessly, mechanically, he was smashed into the foreign casing. And as it was sealed behind him, imprisoning him in it, he lost all awareness.

CHAPTER 12

17 hours

Lightning transfers give great power
But its threads are in my hands.
—Lord of the Jagged Edge

Kierkad was falling. He woke with the ache of a great wailing inside himself that made no detectable sound. He was surrounded by the blackness of space and nothing else.

"… Kierkad respond…. Engage transmitter…. Kierkad respond…"

The strange shapes scattered across a screen in a ticking rhythm, marquee style. He couldn't see it, but it was present at some part of his physical frame. *Tic, tic, tic…*

"… engage transmitter…. Think of that word and make it so…. Kierkad…"

The ticking became letters that coalesced into words with meaning. Wondering how to engage a transmitter and where it would be, Kier made a great effort of will to calm himself, to resist the terror that had afflicted him as he passed out. It was very successful. In fact, he felt himself humming and rippling with electric impulses, glittering interior currents, tiny lightning blazes within him. Intentional thought.

Wow, he thought, and the currents sparkled and flashed within him again. *I will accept transmissions*, he decided and instantly a voice was speaking into his hearing. Not a bilateral resonance detected with two ears, but a digitized mono-source.

"Kierkad, respond," Nirekad's voice was clearly recognizable even in its digital form.

"I'm here," he spoke, and the words were formed directly as digital data and transmitted at the speed of light. "I don't know where here is, or where you are. And I'm falling." He had almost forgotten that since he had calmed himself. The evidence was clear though. He was definitely in free-fall.

"You're in space," the master explained flatly. No emotional tags were added to the data.

"I am aware of space, but I see nothing."

"Open your eyes, Fool," was the reply. "Make it so and you will see."

Kier chose to see and immediately saw on all sides around him at the same time. He was in orbit around the Earth, surrounded by a canopy of stars so thickly populated he could not guess the number, hanging over the vast curvature of the blue planet he had grown to love. Down below he could see all the mountains, valleys, rivers, and roads that made his region. And beyond that, oceans, plains, deserts, and more and more.

Choosing one far away spot, he pressed in to see and found himself zooming in as if he were in the drone, only it was just vision, pressing in till he could detect small animals and flowers.

"Activate scope," Nirekad commanded, and without hesitating, Kierkad obeyed, wheeling around and opening a portal he realized was the 'scope'. "Your mission is to search and destroy the Cascade fleet."

There was no time to ponder the revelation. He wheeled on himself in one plane, then another, clicking and measuring the horizon and the atmosphere below, scouring for a ship. Would he know it when he saw it?

A blip on the edges of the scope caught his attention and with deliberate, fine-tuned movements he positioned his gun precisely and belched a projectile. He had no instrument to measure its sound, and he was unable to track it. After a few moments, a tiny burst of flame and smoke announced the hit.

What did the float ships look like? He wanted to zoom in on one and examine it, see what creature manned it, but the machinery of the satellite he now inhabited was inexorably programmed to perform only a few tasks. 'Search and destroy' was its most urgent.

There were hundreds of blips on the scope. Nearly all moved once he had wheeled into position to lock onto the target. His final tally at the end of what he detected as being 6.235 hours was five projectiles ejected and two hits. There was no conversation with Nirekad the entire time.

He learned what it was to exist without feelings and to move laboriously without impatience. The gun he employed was very effective if the target could be expected to maintain its trajectory while he maneuvered into position, but after the first kill, the fleet was on the alert and able to dodge his targeting device and the projectiles in spite of their basic homing devices. The mechanical movements, the electronic flow of data within the boards and pads, the carefully employed rotations fired by solar charged batteries—it became his mind, his movement, his sense of being.

He existed as a machine.

A panel opened, and a black hole popped him out of the satellite, enveloping him with numbing darkness. There was little fear this time, and the sensation of being drained of life force was tolerable. The long push back to his own frame… no, he wasn't sinking toward the familiar. He was being shunted to another foreign receptacle, a place he didn't want to go. And he fought it without knowing how to fight. The greater system tugged him sideways, funneling him at great speed till he slammed into another body.

Opening his eyes in this vessel, Kier saw he had arms and legs, armored like a Sentinel, and wondered if he were in a form more like his original self, before he had given all to follow the Noble Call. In front of him, another armored body stood.

"Kierkad," the other called, speaking clearly with audible words. "I am Nirekad. This voice is not distinctive."

"Master," Kierkad responded in an identical voice.

The sensation of being in a functional humanoid body, even though it was clearly a robotic one, was an immense relief after the satellite. He could feel gravity and had two eyes and two ears that took in data in the way his brain liked to read it. He still had no feelings, not physical ones, but deep inside, he had a sense of himself, a tiny core that hadn't been lost. He clung to it.

I am me, he thought.

"Come, follow me," Nirekad demanded and turned to walk down a barren, metal passageway. Kierkad followed, matching his footsteps and clumsy gait. It was unavoidable. They were identical models. After several turns and passing through doors, they entered a large room. There were eleven other robots standing there that turned as the two entered.

"Day," one of them greeted.

"New day," Nirekad acknowledged.

It was going to be impossible to tell them apart. But that didn't matter since no one announced their name.

Minor shuffling spaced them all out in a rough circle and one, no different than any other, began the discussion which, as it progressed, was impossible to divide into speakers. They had identical voices, and all faced each other. The anonymity was complete.

"The Cascade has taken three bases in the Delta Sector."

"Fourteen Sentinels have been recruited and are training in Alpha."

"Thirty-six waves of floats have been dropped in the Beta sector in the last twenty-four hours." This voice came from Nirekad on Kier's right.

"Two Cascade ships have been destroyed," Kierkad volunteered, watching to see if anyone would be startled by his contribution, but the discussion simply moved on.

The reports were extensive and extremely confusing. After a while, the monotone voices reporting increasingly tedious numbers and facts had left him dozing with his robotic eyes open, staring into the center of the circle as his mind wandered. He had no idea if the stats added up to great success or huge failure, and he didn't care.

There was no way to track time here, wherever he was, and when it was time to leave, he simply found himself being sucked out of the bot, leaving it there in the room and this time being allowed to sink back into his own body. It felt like a swoon, a pleasant one, falling into a warm and comfortable bed, an immensely relaxing abandon.

Ka-chunk!

The socket repelled his head out of its clutches, and he groaned as leaned forward, unfastening the belts. *Why do these need to be worn?* he thought. His body hadn't moved for many hours, and his limbs were asleep. This was *nothing* like governing the drone that he controlled with his mind while remaining inside his own frame.

I belong here, he thought several times, shaking his arms and legs, trying to stand without leaning on the chair. This receptacle was starving, and greatly in need of sleep, in spite of the long involuntary repose.

"You may eat and sleep," Nirekad informed him as he struggled to lift himself out of his chair. "I cannot speak with you now. But return to me in six hours. It is imperative. Speak to no one else until you have spoken with me."

Kierkad nodded and walked out of the strange room, heading back to the office. The wall hesitated before sliding open, as if he was not permitted to pass, then rolled back a few feet, barely enough to let him through and closed quickly once he had gone out.

Food and sleep. This was all he cared about.

—§—

Sparring. Movements in sync, perfectly timed and balanced, one brother after another stepped up in his dream to match him. Kier fought and twisted, threw and blocked punches, kicked and stopped kicks. It was harmonious and pleasant.

"Well done, Brother," he said as each bout ended.

After several had matched him and stepped aside, one brother came forward and fought very badly. Kier was frustrated by his poor form and interrupted the drill to complain. As he opened his mouth to speak, the brother's features twisted into the mocking face of the subversive he had confronted at that house.

"No!" he cried and began fighting again in earnest, looking for breaks in the opponent's pattern so he would be ready to counter his devices. The battle escalated, the blows coming faster and harder, and still the agent fought him, grinning diabolically. Kier began to grow weary and when he felt himself fading a strange thing happened. A thin, wing-like appendage levered out from his elbow, jagged along the edge, and as he barreled his fist forward into the agent's chest, it landed there, cut through him, and withdrew, slipping back into the slot along the arm. The agent slumped down as Kier grasped his collar and tried to hold him up.

"Stand up, Brother," he demanded, but the figure shrunk, no longer an agent, nor a brother, just a person, muttering gibberish, words that made no sense.

But he wanted them to make sense. "What are you saying? Get up and fight like a Sentinel!" The brother/subversive slid to the floor out of his fingers still murmuring and Kier knelt close to listen.

"… no me…" it said with its last breath.

The dream repeated many times till Kier awoke, but when he got up, he forgot it. Only one thought remained. He had helped to take down a subversive. Perhaps there were many and his victory made little impact, but he knew that their numbers were limited. He had heard that much in the strange robot meeting of minds. Every win counted. And if they were to ask him how many agents of the enemy, how many Cascade operatives he had taken down, he would know what to say.

One.

—§—

"You must speak to no one of the things you have seen or heard and done, Kierkad." Nirekad was leaning forward conspiratorially in his favorite chair by the fire, creating a small cocoon with his presence, figuratively embracing him. "I have placed a great trust in you that you must guard and protect." He leaned back and folded his hands, weaving his fingers together.

"You have seen the map and have met some of the other Pacificators. Of course, many were not there, but we report as we are able and the high counsel of the Order listens and determines how we should proceed." He raised his eyebrows to emphasis the wisdom of the leadership.

Kier, though tired and mentally exhausted, was pining for his daily patrol, his flock, and he didn't care how the Order governed itself. Squelching that feeling, he nodded.

"Now that you are being permitted to ask questions—you must get used to that—I'm surprised you're not asking about the adventure I took you on earlier today." He laughed. "I was astounded the first time I was *transferred*. It was such a…well, a head rush!" He laughed again and this one seemed practiced and timed. It was a speech he had given before.

"Master," Kier replied, realizing a question was now expected. "Why was I sent to a satellite? The work was all programmed and automatic and I could hardly do anything on my own. Wasn't it a long time to be taught a lesson on enemy tactics?" This wasn't quite what he had wanted to ask, but it was safe. His memory of the hours in the satellite, though it had been emotionless at the time, was horrible. And he feared the system that had shoved him into it.

"I see," Nirekad commented with a slight frown. "You thought it unnecessarily long and tedious. I had thought you would complain about the meeting which went on for quite some time." Kier felt him groping at his thoughts and backing away again. Too tired perhaps. "The satellites require human decision to fire and the delay in seeking permission for each target has made them completely useless. It's only recently that one of the Pacificators discovered we could be inserted into the vessel to power the gun. But it's time consuming and we are needed elsewhere."

He looked away for a moment, whispering to himself words he didn't think Kier could pick up. "Unless we find a few subjects docile enough to be able to stay…"

"Where did the meeting take place?" Kier sat stiffly in the chair across from the master, glancing at him when he spoke or when an answer was made, then dropping his eyes to the floor to hide the desperation he felt to get out of there.

"That is not for you to know, not until the day when…if…you rise up to take my place…" He leaned toward Kier again, widening his eyes, raising his eyebrows and his whole forehead. "Yes!" he added, as if this were a great gift. "It is possible. I may advance to become a Darad and join the higher echelon of the Order. And I will need a worthy brother to replace me here."

He closed his eyes and leaned back. "We will see."

Kier couldn't think of anything to say.

"You may go," Nirekad said.

Kierkad rose to his feet and left the room in the normal stride of a Sentinel, resisting the desire to flee, though he couldn't wait to get out of there.

It was late, long past the evening meal, and he knew that the hours he had for sleep were limited. He would soon be on call in the early hours before dawn to fly when the Cascade alarms rang. But he longed for his route. Others would have covered it that morning while he was bound to the orbital gun, but he needed to see that all was well after the confrontation of the night before.

All is well, he wanted to reassure them, and it wasn't enough to know that another Sentinel had communicated the message.

The hangar was dark and silent as he powered up his pod and left the base. Most of the brothers were already resting in their quarters and the few on duty were at their stations around the region.

Kierkad coasted along the quiet roads and willed himself to relax, a normal part of the Indoctriny training. The Harbor was not actively monitoring his activity and showed no indication of wanting to restrict his movements. He was free, for the moment.

There was no wind as he climbed out the door of the pod and began to walk down the street. Lights in windows and the murmur of voices through walls displayed a peaceful and composed setting. The sound of his own footsteps echoed across the yards. Occasionally, a curtain would pull back and someone would peer out to see him walking by. He would wave.

All is well.

Nearing the home of the woman who had asked for help with her system access, he paused. He could hear her voice carrying on a conversation with another person, and a sudden desire to speak with her turned him toward her door. A few quick steps and he was knocking.

The voices inside ceased. He waited. Nothing happened so he knocked again. He didn't want to announce any of the Sentinel commands and frighten her. What could he say instead? He didn't know.

"It's a Sentinel," came the frightened whisper from within, and another long pause.

He knocked a third time and considered opening the door as was his right, but an unlock sequence would be supervised by the Harbor and most likely engage a search for subversives. He didn't want to prove their fear was justified.

"I am here," he said with enough strength they could hear him through the door. "I would like to speak with you."

The door cracked open and the woman with the limp dark hair looked out. "With me?" she asked. Her fear was palpable.

"I will not harm you," Kier said. "You asked for my help yesterday."

"Yes," she faltered, pulling the door open wider, as though she were welcoming her doom, not her guardian. "Come in."

Another woman was standing in the den, crossing her arms tightly, clutching her elbows. She stared at him wide-eyed and said nothing.

Kier stepped across the threshold and pushed aside the restraints of Indoctriny. He steeled himself against the system, if it should decide to awake and pressure him, and let his inner self rise to the surface. He looked into the woman's eyes and appealed to her—he didn't know what he sought. But he felt himself reaching out to her.

Did she detect it? Her eyes reflected sorrow, not the compassion he had hoped for.

"Have you solved your interface problem… Teacher?" he asked awkwardly, striding to the wall where the holo screen would be when activated. The other woman backed away, tripping over the corner of a chair, falling backwards onto the floor, where she scuffled against the far wall and stayed there, gawking.

"No," she answered evenly. "I haven't been able to contact some of my students since I moved here. But don't worry about it…" She bit her lip and looked away, obviously upset.

"What can I do to reassure you and restore your peace?" Kier reached an open hand out to her and the woman at the far wall gasped.

"No!" the teacher took a step back. "I am fine." She glanced at him furtively, her eyebrows creased together. A spark of recognition flashed between them. As if he had seen her before, spoken with her before.

Yesterday, he thought. But confusion churned in the chasm between his surface identity and the under-layer, and a sense of danger began to spread coloring his perception.

"I should go," he announced as he turned and went back out the door. "I apologize for interrupting your evening." The march of a Sentinel led him quick time down the path to the street and on. Behind him he could hear their voices through the walls.

CASCADE

"Oh my God! Oh my God!" the woman sitting on the floor was moaning.

"We better be prepared," the teacher said.

He squelched these words and refused to let them upload to the system. He knew they could be considered evidence of subversion, that they had something to hide, and if the home were searched, it would be his fault.

All is well, he thought, affirming the conclusion strongly, and he continued to reiterate it as he marched. It was easy to see the truth of it.

Except at one place.

Caden's home was dark, and the door hung off its hinges. There was debris scattered in the yard, and the grass was torn and trampled. The crowd in the dark hours before dawn had done more damage than he'd realized. He paused and searched the property. No one was inside. Or perhaps he should look.

Stepping off the sidewalk and moving to the front door of the house became a feat of strength as a surge of power resisted him, suppressing him, insisting that he not go in. But he pushed against it and overcame the barrier.

The house was demolished. Broken furniture, holes in the walls, shattered glass. Everywhere he turned, he saw ruin. It had been utterly destroyed. And in the room where he helped to catch the subversive agent was a pool of dried blood.

Kier ran, as if pursued by the hordes of the Severance and dove into his pod, hurtling away as fast as he could go. But there was no place he could escape the pounding in his chest, and the Harbor was not a refuge any longer.

CHAPTER 13

6 hours

Deception ensnares the people.
We cannot govern them without teaching them lies.
—VanDarad of the first Order of the Jagged Edge

The wailing of the sirens rolled down the road toward him as he neared the hangar. He was not being called to fight, and nothing was sounding in his audio, but he halted the pod and spun it on its axis as the brothers poured out the door in response. Jetting after them, he joined the throng. He would park where they parked and fight where they fought.

He would stay away from Nirekad.

Soaring into the sky in the avatar lacked the exhilaration he had expected, anchored as he was by a strong awareness of his body—a body where he was still residing, maneuvering the craft with his mind—

and its vulnerability. He flew and bobbed over and under gusts of wind, leaning into turns and accelerating out of them, pursuing floats along with the others, but making no attempt to excel.

Who guarded him while he fought in the air? And what would happen if he were attacked while his consciousness was plugged into the drone? When he had been appointed to daylight defense, he would often return to see people gathered around his pod, waiting for a confirmation that he was ok. There was something unnerving about that now.

Kier found himself pulling away from the drone, letting it sink into an auto-decline. *No!* he fought the instinctual retreat, choosing to remain in the avatar. *I will not abandon my brothers in the air*. He would pursue the floats and only land when it was time to chase down the wisps.

The fear that hung over him wasn't coming from the flock. It was the unknown force that had yanked him from his body and crammed him into a machine, without his cooperation or volition. He had been helpless to resist it and unable to even communicate with it. The presence hung over him *now*, whether real or imagined, he didn't know, a massive, brooding entity, heavy on his resting body, waiting there, pressing down, pinning him.

The drone flipped out of control, spinning as if it had collided, and he fought to grip it and compel it to stabilize, directing it along the angle of deviation, dropping in altitude, easing back on the throttle, then pulling up again, climbing, burning fuel. He burst through the cloud cover, cresting the air current that was tossing the floats about as they drifted down, and hovered.

This was not orbit.

He looked around and compared what he could see to what he had seen with the machine sensors in space. Here he felt the humidity and the temperature. He sensed the movements of the air and heard the sound of metallic wings in the distance cutting through floats. He was linked to nature and life, breathing, thinking, experiencing hunger and thirst.

He was alive.

Up there he had been cut off from all that. Existing, but not as a person. Never, never, never again did he want to sit in that chair with a socket for the head.

Now, he knew what the straps were for.

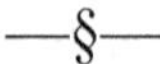

It was in the early predawn hours before he returned to base. Restoration ignored him, and his bed was occupied by another brother. Kier stared at the Sentinel, laying with his arms crossed over his chest, unmoving, completely silent, his breathing barely perceptible. For one terrible, disorienting moment, he thought he had been knocked out of himself and was staring at his own body, unable to return, homeless, untethered, and lost. Then the emblem on his forearm throbbed in a dull orange glow and he dropped his eyes to look at it, and knew he was himself.

I am Kierkad, he thought.

The other Sentinel's armor hung charging where his would be. The realization came to him that he had fought in the wrong shift and had missed the hours he should be sleeping. His bed was occupied.

Perhaps another was empty.

Roaming through the halls, wandering down the quiet corridors on several floors, he found only rooms with sleeping brothers. Not one was available. He didn't know what to do. He had never lacked a place to sleep before.

Humans could lay down anywhere and close their eyes. *Perhaps I can also.* Since his pod was the only place that was truly his own, he returned to it and drove out to his usual spot. It felt strange to park and fold his arms across his chest without launching into the avatar. But he reminded himself, *I am unsteady from lack of sleep*, knowing this would make collisions more likely.

Closing his eyes, he fell almost instantly into a deep sleep and dreamed of battle.

He fought the Cascade in the skies and on the land. He tramped through houses and busted open doors and caught subversives in the very act of sabotage. He whirled on several planes in orbit around the Earth, whipping and pummeling the Cascade fleet, targeting, rotating, projecting missiles at breathtaking speeds, knocking out one after another in rapid succession. He flew and flamed through floats and crushed chips between his fingertips.

Except for one.

The tumult of war ceased as he held up this one to look at and recognized it. The boy's chip, mere aluminum etched in pencil, so easy to crumple. *The box had this code.* He pondered it and groped for the key to open it. Hadn't he already opened the box? What had it said?

When he had been fighting and chips would dash against his drone spitting their data, he had taken in streams and streams of digital gibberish, the same message repeating over and over again. None of it had ever made sense. But for the first time, he noticed the *shape* it described.

It was a shape. An idea of a place. Not a box—a room!

The thought was so jarring, Kier flung himself against the roof of his pod with a loud cry, jolting fully awake. He climbed out of the pod, shaking and looking around in the dark.

What does it mean?

Did the chips identify a place? Was this real or the madness of a sleeping mind? He began pacing back and forth along the street near his pod. There was a clear impression of a room inside a house in his mind. And it wasn't the first time this had come to him. He thought it had been an arbitrary image from a dream, built from sparse memories of the homes he had helped to build. But when the boy had planted him with that childish version of a chip, the two ideas became linked. He had thought he would find that room when he entered Caden's home.

Why would a subversive end up there? It made no sense. Unless...it hadn't been the right room.

Kier stood still and lifted his eyes to gaze down the street at the homes he patrolled every day. Searching with his heart as well as his infrared, he longed for something. He ached for it. But he didn't know what it could be.

"Sentinel, report," came the command through his audio, detecting his lack of activity. Was it the Harbor or the Pacificator that had noticed he was out of place? He hesitated. A response was expected.

"Nothing to report," he said. He wasn't linked into the battle audio feed though he could hear the whirring of the wings overhead as the drones fought. If he knew what to do, he had a little time to act.

The teacher came to mind. Her behavior was odd. The image of the room surfaced so strongly within him that he was suddenly convinced that her house was the one he should search. She was either a subversive agent, or…in danger. If one Sentinel, Kierkad, had identified her home as a threat, others would too.

Even now she could be facing a Sentinel clothed in anger. The thought chilled his blood.

Kier sprung from the ground with a leap, powered with all the strength his legs could impel, and hit the pavement running toward the house with the blue shutters, pounding the road, sending faint tremors to the homes he passed, stirring sleeping occupants, troubling some who lay awake tossing. An expanding wake of anxiety spread behind him.

He wanted to yell but had no words. The blocks were longer than he remembered. The home farther than he had realized. He leaned into the wind and ran harder and faster with every stride, hurdling objects, curbs, and holes. Finally, he was near enough to see the home and determine that it was not yet under siege.

He stopped and bent over, panting, bracing himself with his hands against his knees. He must still be very tired to be winded by a sprint like that. Straightening and continuing his approach at a more leisurely pace, he breathed deeply and calmed himself.

He could go to the door again and ask to see the room. Or he could wait outside to watch for his brothers. Or he could plug into the battle audio feed and join the search for wisps.

He looked up and over his shoulder where the drones were beginning to land and considered joining the hunt on land. The fewer chips they encountered, the less likely they would decipher the code and find this house.

But his heart drew him. The tug toward that room was so strong he could hardly bear to resist. Turning back but not moving, he waited, thinking about the longing, afraid and yet desperate to follow it. His chest moved first, under a magnetic pull, in the direction of the house, only half a block away.

But he was arrested by two Sentinels who grasped him on either side.

"You are out of Order," one said, holding him in a vice-like grip.

"You are commanded to return to Pacificator Nirekad's office," the other articulated, speaking for Nirekad himself, Kier was certain.

They whipped him around and inserted him deftly into his pod which they had brought with them and coded an auto-return sequence. Kier didn't resist them and didn't try to explain. It was pointless.

He sunk into the seat, closing his eyes and quieted the ache in his chest, and was asleep again before he reached the Harbor.

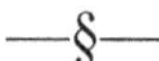

Two Sentinels dragged him from his pod once it came to a rest in the hangar and propelled him down the passageways toward the Pacificator's chambers, though he would have walked there in his own strength without their coercion. Depositing him, they turned and marched away. Nirekad was nowhere in sight, so Kier waited for him standing at attention. It occurred to him that the emblem, though still pulsing in the normal way, had applied no pressure and he hadn't been dosed or disciplined according to the usual procedure. There was no indication that Nirekad was fumbling around in his mind either.

I need to hide my thoughts about the room and the teacher, he advised himself, stuffing them deeper and replacing them with a tumble of memories about his latest battles with the Cascade.

Another Sentinel was brought in by two brothers and shoved near him. This one didn't stand at attention. He looked around, noticed Kier, and moved toward the table.

"It never changes," he commented, staring at the map, still stretched out as it had been the day before. "I wonder if there's any truth in it at all."

"The valleys and roads are familiar," Kier ventured, stepping up next to him, glancing at his face and then pouring over the map, exploring every detail, trying to connect what he had seen from orbit with what was displayed here.

"No," Mevkad said. That was who had been brought in after him. "I've seen the earth from out there and it didn't look like this."

"So did I, and it did look like this." Kier wondered why he would lie about it.

"You were in the machine?" Mevkad turned on him in shock. "They did that to you, too? Why? Why did he send us there?" His hand trembled where it rested on table. "I haven't been the same since that day." He shook his head and looked away.

"Early this morning," Kier said, stretching a hand and pointing toward the regions he recognized. "I saw these places from up there, but there was more beyond, curving away around the edge of the planet."

"I must have been on a different side," Mevkad said, raising his forearm to his chest and resting the emblem there against the skin, calming himself. "He did not lie to me. Maybe I am confused or deceived in some way, but it was not intentional cruelty. He wasn't trying to hurt me…"

"Brother," Kier placed a hand on his shoulder. "You are not well. Have you been restored?"

Mev lifted his eyes and looked into Kier's face. "You are the brother who looked at me…like you can see me, but no one can see me. I don't know why you look at me like that."

It was disturbing.

"I see you have made good use of the time," Nirekad said as he entered from the back room, the hidden door sliding into the wall behind him. He joined them at the map table, standing on the opposite side. Kier felt his return at the edges of his mind as well and was glad he had hidden his other thoughts. Nirekad stared at him for few moments and then fixed his gaze on Mevkad.

"That house you were trying to enter," Nirekad said, sending a shudder down Mevkad's back. "What were you looking for there? Why did you want to enter that one in particular?"

"No!" Mevkad resisted weakly. "I don't know. Don't make me think about it. Don't look at it!" He crossed both arms over his chest in the sleeping position, though he was standing, clinging to his arms, scrunching his face, and closed his eyes.

"Come, Mevkad," Nirekad spoke with a hint of kindness, making his voice resonate as it did when he spoke to all the brothers. "Kierkad, if you would?" He held his hand toward Mevkad and raised his eyebrows to Kier, asking for help to get him moving.

Kier laid his hand on Mevkad's shoulder again and applied a little pressure to move him, directing him to the other side of the table, toward Nirekad, who backed away waving with his arms, drawing them on. He led them slowly to the hidden door, Mevkad with reluctant steps, Kier with foreboding.

CASCADE

"Wait!" Mevkad cried out opening his eyes as they passed through into the hall. "I don't want to go in there again!" He planted his feet and wouldn't budge, blocking the door so it couldn't close.

His fear triggered an anger response in Kierkad. Rage started rumbling in his torso. His armor began to darken as he turned to look at the master. Drawing himself up taller, "Stand down!" he ordered, extending an arm in the master's direction.

Nirekad was startled and shaken by the reaction. "Kierkad, you are out of Order!" he bellowed but his voice lacked the assurance of command.

"Stand down, Sentinel!" Kierkad insisted, stepping forward and leaning into his face, not quite bringing his fist to the Pacificator's chest.

"Yes, Brother!" Nirekad wisely conceded, backing away. "Let's go back out into my office. Mevkad will be safe there. Come! Sentinel, disengage." He slipped around Kierkad and pulled the other brother with him, retreating out of arm's reach.

Kierkad swiveled, keeping his fist pointed his direction, until he sensed Mevkad's fear diminishing. Then he dropped his arm to his side. His armor began to lighten and his head to clear. He took a few deep breaths.

"Kierkad," Nirekad resumed his air of authority again now that the rage had passed. "It is forbidden to become angry at your Master! You must restrict this!" It was his turn to be angry.

Mevkad was watching Kier's face, studying it as if he recognized him from another time, another place. "Do I know you?" he asked, desolate words echoed by shadows in his eyes. He didn't believe it, but wished it were true.

Do you know me? Kier wanted to counter, but Nirekad was absorbing it all too avidly for him. "I sparred with you in town two nights ago…" Or was it three? It seemed a long time since that night.

"But tonight, you are defending me. You saw my fear… there's danger down there." He gestured toward the wall, now closed.

"It was a kindness. An unnecessary one, but kind. This is what it means to be brothers. We love one another." Nirekad hurried through the words, tired of the interruption. "Kierkad," he went on, "You must perform a mission for me. I need someone I can trust…" His voice conveyed no trust at all, and Kier felt the master's desire to get rid of him.

The Pacificator projected the charge into the Harbor system, and the command came through Kier's emblem. Snapping to attention, Kierkad nodded and marched out without a word.

Behind him he could hear his brother, Mev, calling out. "I won't forget, Kier. You saw…"

Two other Sentinels met him in the hall and came alongside, keeping pace as he made his way back to the pods once again. The destination was clearly marked in his visuals, and the urgency drove them at top speed.

Nirekad had sent them to the neighborhood where Mevkad had turned on his brothers and lost his Order, where he had fought and Kier had taken him down. They returned to the very house and yard where the fight had taken place. Suddenly, Kier understood that the location had been vivid in Mevkad's mind as a place of importance, a place he wanted to visit. A secret place where a sliver of hope abided.

Just like Kier.

CASCADE

With a sense of horror, he saw the Sentinels barge up to the door and ran to place himself in front of them. They could NOT be allowed into the house first.

"Stand Down, Sentinels!" he shouted. "This is my charge, and I am in command!" They stepped aside and waited obediently for him. He hoped the commotion would wake the inhabitants and give them fair warning of the search.

Kierkad knocked. "Sentinel search!" he called as he cracked the door open. Frantic scuffles inside rewarded him. "Do not harm the flock!" he ordered, turning to the two Sentinels at his side.

They pushed past him and began to tear the room apart, breaking open walls, smashing anything and everything, oblivious of the screams down the hall. Kierkad barred the way to give the people time to escape out the back and hoped they would get out in time.

We used to be guardians. He longed for the days when this part of the Sentinel's call had been unknown to him, when there were no subversive agents or reasons to destroy someone's home. The ache in his chest began to throb again painfully.

The Sentinels rammed into him when they had thoroughly ransacked the front rooms of the house and insisted on getting to the bedrooms. Kierkad gave way reluctantly, only budging when he could not prevent it and they steamrolled their way to the first door, ripping it off its hinges.

Kier was astonished at the rabid fury they exhibited and the extent of the damage they wrought. Finally, he saw that Nirekad had decided not just to ransack a home where an agent might be hidden, one who was trying to lure a Sentinel into his trap. He wanted to destroy any hope Mevkad had left. The hope of something else…something nameless that pulled on his heart and filled him with longing…the hope of escaping the life of a Sentinel.

Kierkad walked out of the house and left it to the dogs to ravage.

CHAPTER 14

2 hours

Take up weapons but beware
The blade kills friend and foe alike
—An old proverb

Kier found himself in his room, staring at the sleeping Sentinel on his bed with no memory of how he got there. His hands were shaking. Intense emotion coursed through his limbs, a great tempest demanding action, and nowhere to unleash it. Breathing heavily, blinking to clear his vision, Kier moved behind the bed and knelt by the wall.

With trembling fingers, he traced the cracks in the concrete block wall. One crevice was familiar. He instructed a blade to extend from concealment in his arm-plate—making for the first time an intentional choice. Three blades protruded, one sliding down from the upper arm, another levering down at the elbow, and the third, poking out at the wrist. Black, vicious looking things with jagged edges.

Retract, he commanded two of them, keeping only the wrist blade out. Sliding it into the crack, he deftly snagged and extricated a folded piece of paper, browning on the sides and corners. He rose slowly to a stand and unfolded it, while the third blade disappeared into the armor.

His memory had been a poor-resolution facsimile of the real picture. The original was more detailed and vivid. The crayon lines were textured by the paper they had colored on. The people running away were not just anonymous human shapes, they had distinctive features that a child could recognize. One was a man with glasses and dark green hair with mad eyebrows and a threatening grimace. There was a woman with curls pulling on a little girl in a pink dress who was hiding her face. The small boy in the center of the drawing was sitting on the floor with toy animals, staring at the monster, his mouth a wide circle.

The creature was a dark hulking thing with multiple limbs hanging over the child, with several levered appendages hanging from both limbs. A Sentinel, clothed in the colors of anger. The crayon sketched him in black and red dripped from his limbs.

I am the beast, Kier thought to himself in horror. And the one hope this picture had always held for him, that he had rescued the boy, was dashed. The Order demanded that no child ever be injured, but there was nothing he could trust in anymore.

Not even himself.

"Brother," the Sentinel on the bed sat up abruptly, dropping his legs over the side and hopping to a stand next to him, yanked from a sound sleep to serve the system. "Report to the Pacificator's office. You will be escorted."

Kier jumped to his feet and strode out before the brother could clap a rigid hand on his shoulder, determined this time to go of his own free will. "I am responding immediately," he said. The Sentinel reached out to grab him but didn't quicken his steps to make up the difference and Kier was able to keep just out of reach. It was a small thing, this tiny act of independence, but it strengthened him.

"Kierkad," Nirekad was standing with his back to the fireplace, hands folded together, glaring at him in disapproval. "You were to return to me as soon as the subversives were dealt with. Yet you detoured. It is not your time for sleep!"

Kierkad looked at the master, unable to hide the despair he felt. "You know what we are," he almost choked over the words, stretching out the picture to him, showing it to him. "There is no difference between the guardian and the beast."

"Where did you get that?" Nirekad took it from his hand and studied it, murmuring under his breath. "Yes…yes…" his words became audible. "I see what this is. Clever of you to hide it for so long."

"I kept it, but I have not been able to understand it until now." Kier glanced around the room, noticing the slight change in the darkness outside. Dawn was approaching.

Time was advancing.

"Well, I will overlook the subterfuge…it was time for you to know anyway." Nirekad beckoned with an outstretched hand and Kier obeyed, coming close. There was no comfort in his proximity or the conspiratorial manner in which he spoke next. He had become a foul thing in Kier's mind.

"Come, Brother, it is time to grow up." The Pacificator put his arm around Kier's shoulder and leaned close to his ear to speak softly. "You are a child no longer. There is nothing to fear."

The words collided against his ears and wouldn't enter his mind. They were clumsy sounds. "I am not afraid," he said, standing stiffly, staring into the fire.

"The Sentinel is a guardian in more ways than one." Nirekad directed him with a gentle pressure along his back, turning him toward the far wall, moving him one step at a time. "Protecting the flock from danger, interrupting human quarrels, rescuing children from unhappy homes…" He let the last sentence hang in the air for a moment.

"You are saying this picture shows an unhappy home." Kier saw only the terror of the Sentinel's invasion.

"You were too young to understand at the time that it was a rescue. But now," Nirekad nodded. He was using his most kind and warm voice, the one that made the brothers feel loved. The one that used to mean something. "You are able to grasp the danger that every human child faces. You battle it day and night…"

Too young. Reverberating in his head, these words jarred and jolted him. *I have been young.* Time rolling forward revealed itself to him with this one thought. The progress of time, every day, every year, every hour—it all progressed from this one day.

This day. He looked down at the picture in Nirekad's hand.

I am the child.

He paused in their slow movement forward with one foot across the doorway into the hidden hall. Looking Nirekad full in the face, he burrowed into his eyes, scanning for what might be there. The emblem on his arm pulsed and throbbed and he sensed that he was using it, projecting outward toward the master of the system.

"Ah!" Nirekad grinned widely. "Aha!! You are learning quickly! You crave the knowledge I can give you!!" He pushed on Kier's back to keep him moving him down the passageway, but he wouldn't budge.

Kier found himself groping along the system lines, sensing brothers sleeping, others eating, some preparing for their patrols. None were fighting the Cascade at that moment.

Nirekad was laughing.

"Here!" he exulted, "Let me help you!" Grabbing Kier's right arm, he pulled it up to the top of his head and pressed the emblem against his scalp where his own mark of the Sentinel pulsed in green and blue. Both of Kier's marks immediately synced and pulsed with the same colors, on his arm and at his chest-plate.

The contact blasted him with a flood of sight and knowledge he was unable to contain, bowling him over, rolling him around, tossing him like surf. So many places, people, processes, maps, plans, devices. All over the earth and in orbit around the planet were a multitude of factors, bases, weapons… and other Pacificators. He could detect them in the distance, scattered around the Sentinel regions. And they were all linked to a deeper, thicker realm, where higher powers resided, Conciliators and their network of members stretched in a tight web. One massive seat at the very center was unoccupied.

"There! There!" Nirekad burst out excitedly. "The seat is finally empty, and the Conciliators are choosing a successor. One of them will rise to rule and one of us will ascend to take the place that opens up. It must be me! I must ascend!!" He was pushing Kier harder now and Kier was yielding, taking one reluctant step after another, caught up in the glut of information pouring over him.

Nirekad would become NireDarad and Kierkad would be Pacificator. He could see it clearly. He would have the authority to govern the brothers at the Harbor, for healing, for teaching, for restoration. He could soften their tactics among the humans while honing their skills against the Cascade.

A new wave washed over him. *The Cascade!* Code designed to disrupt the Sentinels and destroy their links to the Order! He could see it now, the high threat it posed, and understood that detaching a Sentinel destroyed him. He couldn't live apart from the system. The subversives were everywhere—he saw their mocking shapes manning Cascade ships releasing thousands of floats from high in the atmosphere— masquerading as people, covering their true nature.

But Kier noticed how childish the picture of their faces appeared. It struck him as odd that they were identical and all grinned in the same way. It had a familiar quality to it, as if someone had imagined those faces by looking in a mirror making evil expressions.

It was invented.

Kier suspected Nirekad himself had done so.

"The subversives," he muttered, stumbling forward, tripping over something. He caught himself on the arms of a chair. Nirekad had guided him back to that room with the column. "No..." he mumbled, realizing at the same moment that he had been dosed and his body had little strength to resist.

But he wasn't completely helpless. He wrestled sluggishly with the master, trying to shove him back and escape the room. Nirekad was older and weaker, and lacked armor to strengthen him, but he was a match for Kierkad in his drugged state. They fought like two old men with slow clumsy blows and parries.

Nirekad relished the battle, announcing his every move with cries, cackles, and guttural yells. He looked fiendishly happy. Kier knew from the glimpse he had had of the master's mind that he missed combat and the physical sensation of breaking things. He rode closely on the Sentinel's feed when he sent them to destroy homes.

One foot. Nirekad managed to thrust Kier's leg against the chair and trigger a clamp at the same time. It caught him painfully, forcing him to stand as it tightened on his ankle. The fight grew more savage now as Nirekad brought his full weight against him pressing him into the seat, taking every blow Kier dealt without bothering to deflect it, grunting with the impact.

One arm. Kier was pinned on one full side now, scrambling to fling the assailant backward and flip himself over the side of the chair. But his head was spinning, and nausea was setting in.

Out of the corner of his eye he caught sight of another brother fastened into one of the chairs, unmoving, pale as death itself. Mevkad.

My Brother! he thought in anguish, remembering Mev's fear of this place and his last words to Kier. Why would Nirekad want to imprison both of them in the chairs? Nirekad might be forcing Kier into some kind of interrogation at the hand of the other Pacificators, some kind of induction, before he could be considered for leadership at the base. But Mevkad hadn't been offered anything.

*A few subjects docile enough to stay...*Nirekad had said. He wanted to plug Mev into a satellite and leave him there!

"No!" Kier cried out, hesitating for only a second, and Nirekad slammed his other foot into the clamp. He climbed onto his lap, gripped both armrests and pushed with all his strength, smashing Kier down into the chair, battling the final free arm.

A burst of adrenaline from somewhere deep within, powered by rage, pumped Kier's body. Growling and gritting his teeth, he lashed out with his unfettered fist, pummeling the master.

Nirekad didn't back off or let go. He pressed his head into Kier's neck and one knee into his chest, fighting to pin Kier's arm with both hands.

When the brothers were forced to undergo harmonizing, pressed against each other, overcome with rage, their armor crashed and rattled, filling the hall with noise that gradually synced into a rhythm. This was nothing like that. The noise filled the room, but it never synced or calmed. It grew more desperate with each minute that passed.

Kier saw the master was bleeding from some of the blows he had taken and realized what he had neglected.

Extend, he thought, commanding all the blades on both arms to engage. His left arm was pinned in a clamp and the blades dug into the chair around it, one of them laying its edge against his armor, expanding and threatening to crack the plate.

Nirekad screamed as the other arm exposed its weapons. Kier's wrist blade pierced his bare arm and the levered blade snapped open slicing at his leg with its jagged edge. The third poked into the air. Now all Nirekad's focus was on avoiding those blades.

Kier wrapped his free arm around the master, blades pressing against the skin of his face and chest, pinning him into his lap. Just as he felt the scrape of clamps at his neck, Kier jerked and stunned the old man with a head-slam. Nirekad's body slumped and began to slide down to the floor as the socket behind Kier's head sucked and rattled its clamps, searching for the head that had come so close.

Kier retracted his blades and reached over to unfasten the clamps. Standing up shakily, he turned to look at the chair. There was a clamp at the waist that, if activated, would have been impossible to escape, and he wondered why the master hadn't triggered it.

Nirekad lay groaning on the floor. Kier reached under his arms and grabbed him around the chest, lifting him off the floor and settling him in the chair he had just escaped. He fastened his arms and legs into the clamps and shoved him back against the seat to engage the waist clamp. But he held his head forward, not wanting him to escape into that greater system where the Pacificators met.

He panted and noticed for the first time that his armor was dark, the color of anger.

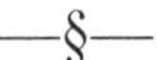

The blue planet spread out in a vast panorama beneath the satellite, curving toward the east and the west, the north and the south. Banks of clouds swirled lazily around massive stretches of ocean and the edge of night crept along the ground, arching from one end to the other, as daylight advanced a centimeter at a time, valleys lit up, and inhabitants began to stir.

The spread of space enveloping the earth, was filled with a profusion of stars, glittering against its dark canopy. Orbiting lifelessly in a band around the planet, lost in a scattered collection of obsolete mechanisms, was an aging satellite. Its solar panels barely functioning, and its movement capabilities restricted by broken or missing parts. Its supply of ammunition was limited, and its backup fuel would soon be spent.

It was a dying object.

It rotated on one axis with slow clicks, then on another, and its scope sighted movement down below, toward the surface. It latched onto a flying ship, tracked it, armed a projectile, and waited until the target was out of reach. Then it continued clicking and turning on itself, sighting and identifying, watching and preparing to launch, only to back down each time.

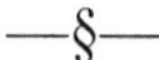

Kier wanted to release Mevkad but didn't know how the system worked and what would happen if he pulled him out without summoning his mind back first. *Nirekad knows*, he thought, laying his right arm over the master's head, holding it up and connecting with the mark at the same time.

Floods of information sloshed up against him, threatening to tumble him again, but he found his footing and resisted the weight of it. He clung to his identity within himself. *I am Kier*, he thought. And from this position, he explored.

He searched for records of Mevkad and saw his life shoot into vision, streaming past the days up until a few days ago, pausing to look at the record of the fight from the Harbor's perspective, collected from the brothers, including Kier, who had fought him, and from Mevkad himself. It was fascinating to view all the data at the same time and understand each brother's angle. But he couldn't waste any time. He sped up to see the most recent events and found the moments after his departure. It had been a simple thing for the master to instruct the system to dose Mevkad so he could usher him down the hall into the transfer chair. He had buckled him in, shoved his head backed into the socket, and placed his hands on the dome. It had activated and Mevkad had been sucked out of his body.

The transfer trajectory looked like a golden line shooting up from the ground into space and he could see that a miniature, luminescent globe had hurtled through it and been folded onto itself, corner by corner, and packed into one of the machines, like the one Kier had been crammed in.

A tiny, silvery thread still stretched back all the way to this chair. Mevkad was still alive.

Kier continued searching the records, looking for a way to extract him safely, and it occurred to him that he was in grave danger the moment Nirekad awoke. Even if he could rescue his brother, the entire Harbor system was at Nirekad's command. How would they avoid being subjected to whatever torment would follow?

But…if he were to replace Nirekad, he could protect his brother. In fact, cooperating with Nirekad might be the best way to do so.

Kier decided on a different tactic. He dug down into Nirekad's mind, which was easier than combing through the Harbor's records. He sensed the master was stirring and the groping in his thoughts would wake him faster. *How can I release Mevkad?* he demanded, and the process opened to him, how to lay his hands on the dome and bring it to life.

But it was already activated.

Nirekad had wakened it and left it running so that when he plugged Kier in, he would immediately be extracted and sent...sent where? The destination eluded him. Nirekad was alert enough to resist him.

Kier backed out of his mind and dove into the Harbor again. Where? What were the destinations this thing controlled?

You can take his place and protect your brother.

A chill ran through Kier as he realized another mind was touching his. One he didn't know. It reached forward and pulled on him, experienced at communicating within the bounds of the Order.

It is time for you to ascend, it said.

Kier withdrew and it followed. He sunk down into his own mind, and it pursued him there.

I have been watching you, Kier.

It was like being cornered in his pod, with the door blocked by an entity that was bigger, stronger, and had the power to paralyze him.

Let me show you, it whispered enticingly. Vivid images, larger and more brilliantly colored than life, portrayed Kierkad the Pacificator ruling over the Harbor, uttering the moving speeches in the hall, overseeing the care of the brothers and the guardianship of the human flock. He saw himself consulting with other wise Sentinels, handsome, noble, eyes filled with idealism looking into the distant future—building that future in the present. He felt an intoxicating rush of the pride of ruling and the arrogance of being superior to his predecessor. He would be noticed by the inner circle, spoken of, commended. He would rise one day, ahead of all of them, to be the One leader.

He felt it all in an instant and the craving for it overwhelmed him. Everything wrong could be set right. All of it.

As the vision faded, Kier thought of Mev, crammed into metal, alone in space. *How can I recover my Brother?* he pleaded.

A flash of wrath from the Mind scalded his soul. *I see the room*, it said.

With a cry of horror, Kier jumped to his feet, yanking his arm away from the master's head, severing the emblem connection.

Nirekad's head dropped backward, and the socket clamped onto it with a loud sucking sound and his whole body went limp in a way it hadn't been before.

Like death.

CHAPTER 15

24 Minutes

Love is worth the cost.
—The Cascade

Kier rushed to Mevkad, detached all the clamps and belts that held him in place and searched for a way to bring him back. There were no switches or buttons he could detect, and he dared not try accessing the Harbor again through Nirekad's mark.

The mark of the Sentinel. The Harbor's access point. Kier pressed the emblem on his forearm against Mev's arm and pressed into the system against the flow. He found the tracking sensors monitoring the base, brothers sleeping, eating, patrolling. This was all he could see when he had tried to read Nirekad but hadn't been in physical contact with him. He couldn't reach Mev's signal at all.

He opened his eyes, stared at Mev's deadpan face for a moment, then shifted his gaze to the mark on his arm. *Find this Sentinel!* he ordered.

The Harbor responded. It led him along a string of digital veins, bypassing multiple branches, taking some turns, pausing and rejecting others. It settled on one spot. An empty port.

Kier was puzzled at first until he realized this was the very socket Mev had been plugged into when he was transferred. Frantically, he ransacked the data stored there, looking for clues, and then in desperation, he sent a call through the port, a single pulse with his brother's name. Mev. It sparked its way off at the speed of light.

But there was no answer.

Kier pulled away, glancing quickly at Nirekad to confirm that he was still locked into place.

The words of the other Mind pierced him. The room, it had said … *The* room. The one Kier hadn't wanted anyone to discover, where the message of the chip had led him.

The room in the teacher's house.

I must protect her! Kier twisted and just as he was about to run out, Mev's voice called out to him weakly.

"Brother!" he whispered. "I am weak. Help me rise out of this chair."

"Mev!" Kier cried, jumping back to his side, wondering why the Mind had relented. "How did you get back? Did you hear me call? Where were you?"

"I know, I know," Mevkad said, leaning forward, rubbing his head and laying a hand over the emblem on his forearm, an involuntary movement. Kier paused at that. It was off somehow. It reminded Kier of something he couldn't put his finger on. "I came back," he added.

"Are you alright?" Kier pulled his gaze away from Mev's arm and searched his face.

"Help me stand. He drugged me and I can barely move."

Kier snaked an arm under his shoulder and around his back and lifted him to his feet. "Wait," Mevkad said, breathing and focusing on the floor. "Let me get my bearings." Kier waited, though the delay pained him. He didn't know how much time he had to get to the teacher's house to warn her.

When he was steadier, Mevkad took a couple steps leaning on Kier, not toward the door, but back toward Nirekad's body, pinned helplessly in the chair. He chuckled softly and sneered at him.

Kier hadn't known Mev very well, but he *knew* this was out of character.

Mevkad pushed away from Kier, stood upright, and took a step on his own. He leaned over Nirekad's body, and a chill ran through Kier's heart making it leap into his throat. Before he could think what to do or even move a muscle, Mevkad grabbed the emblem embedded on Nirekad's head and ripped it off, bringing with it strips of dead skin and shreds of gray hair, barely a drop of blood on it. Then he calmly scraped it clean with his fingers, wiped it on the old master's robes, and pressed it to the top of his own head.

Kier backed away a step without taking his eyes off him.

As the emblem began to glow blue and green, Mevkad turned to face Kier, grinning broadly. "Oh, it's good!" he said. "It's good to be here!"

Kier took another step backward.

"I had thought about taking your vessel, but you turned out to be the clever one, so I let you remain."

He stretched out his arm and extended the levered blade, turned to Nirekad's body and stabbed it where it lay, right through the chest. Rotating back, Mevkad smiled at Kier. "It is done," he said, "I have passed the test. I am now a Conciliator. You may address me as MevDarad."

Kier stared at his former master.

"You can still be Pacificator," MevDarad said, "I meant that. There's only one obstacle that must be dealt with first."

Would he have to fight him to escape? He had bested Mevkad before, and perhaps the former master, now the Conciliator, wouldn't have any added skill, and he still had drugs in his body. But when he saw the jagged edge of the blade and understood that MevDarad wore the armor of a Sentinel, one who would fight to kill without remorse, he realized it was pointless.

He had to escape and warn the teacher before it was too late.

Wait! Kier's thoughts hooked back to what the master had just said. *What obstacle?*

"The room," MevDarad said.

Of course, he was reading his mind.

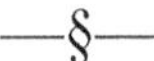

Cascade fleet ships were soaring through the skies dropping their payloads in strategic places over the realms of the Sentinels and the satellite that watched them did nothing to stop them. It scanned with its scope, latching on when they came within range, focused and targeted, rotating in one, then a second, and then a third plane, until it was precisely in position to fire. It would rearm the projectile, start a countdown, pause the countdown, and wait. Then the ship would zip out of range, and it would cancel the countdown, disarm the projectile, and begin searching again.

Mev had learned one override to pause the automatic sequence. Now he combed through the internal structures looking for another.

—§—

Kier fled the hidden room, burst out of the opening in the wall, tore through the master's chambers, and raced through the halls toward the hangar. Sentinels were striding up and down hallways, intent on their various tasks, accessible to Nirekad—he couldn't think of him as MevDarad—at any time, but no one stopped him.

"Run!" a voice came to him over his audio. "You will lead us to it. They always do. You can't help it."

Kier dove into his pod and shot out the exit recklessly at high velocity, not caring any more how many Sentinels were sent after him. Every second counted. Every instant mattered. Even if he could not protect the house and the room, he might be able to save the teacher.

The stars were beginning to fade as the light from around the edge of the horizon filtered through the atmosphere. Dawn was approaching. The streets were empty and the ranks battling the Cascade were far away, out of sight and earshot. Kier's pace across town sent him careening around corners, narrowly avoiding trees and fences, and he reached the teacher's home faster than he had thought possible.

He dove out yelling. "Awake! Awake, neighbors!" he cried out as he pounded up to the front door. He pounded on the door. "Danger! You must flee!" and he could hear Nirekad laughing in the background.

"I am sending reinforcements, Kierkad," MevDarad's voice informed.

Kier pounded the door again and then opened it. People were spilling into the streets behind him, gathering around the house at a safe distance, watching. He knew this would restrain the Sentinels who would soon arrive. That would improve the teacher's chances to slip away out the back.

"You!" the teacher's voice came down the hall as she came toward him, wrapped in a bulky sweater, "Why are you here? What's wrong?" Her eyes were afraid but there was something else there too that he couldn't place.

"No, no, no!" Kier begged her, shoving her backward. "You've got to get out of here!"

"Okay, okay!" she raised her hands, palms out toward him as if to hold him back. "I will, but you…"

"The room!" Kier's voice grated as he tried to mask the words so that only she would understand. "They think there's a room in your house where the Cascade…"

"What room?" she whispered, backing away from him toward the door *he knew* led to it. "What room?"

"It's because of me…. I made up this idea…it's wrong…. It's all wrong…" He pressed toward her as she backed away. He could hear her heart beating fast and see the intensity in her face. *Why didn't she just run?*

"This room?" she whispered, leaning with her back against the door, reaching behind her with a hand to turn the knob.

And the door swung open.

Mission objective, read the header. **Find and eliminate enemy ships.**

Descriptions followed.

The satellite erased the mission objective. How could it create a new one for itself? The acts of will that had been needed to pause the countdown, search for the command center, and erase the mission objective were debilitating. Mev had disabled the assignment that had been thrust upon him but now he had nothing, no purpose or reason to exist.

He sat inactive for a span of time. He wasn't sure how long. Then it occurred to him that he might be able to access the Harbor or one of the Sentinels and ask for help. Initiating a choice within his core, he activated the audio receiver. There was no working transmitter that he could find.

Voices of the brothers began to pour in. He tuned the frequency looking for his own base and found the Harbor. A great battle was just beginning that stirred mild curiosity.

He listened.

The entire complement of Sentinels was being mobilized to pursue subversive agents in town. They were highly dangerous and extreme measures were allowed. "Encouraged." This last word was inserted by a voice he recognized as his own.

He understood. He knew what the master had done.

He had been severed. He was lost.

Multiple voices updated one another as the Sentinels ran to their pods and jetted out the hangar. Updates from the Harbor were being called out by the brothers to one another. One of these announcements stood out.

"Sentinel Kierkad is out of Order and considered highly dangerous."

Mev remembered how Kier had stood up for him the last time he had seen him. He had believed until then that he was alone. But his brother had shown him otherwise.

You are not alone either, Mev thought, as he encoded his new mission objective.

The teacher backed into the room and Kier followed. "Quick!" she shrieked, and the door slammed shut behind him. Someone lodged a heavy metal bar across it.

"Kierkad, listen to me," the woman spoke hoarsely, urgency mixed with anxiety tinging her words. "They can't hear you right now. But there's no time to explain. This is your last chance! There won't be any others!" Her words grew in pitch toward the end, desperation driving them up in a crescendo.

Kier whipped around to see the other woman behind him. She had barred the door, now she stood there weeping, wringing her hands, moving sideways along the wall to get to the far side of the room. She was shaking her head at him, no, no, no, no.

He turned back to look at the teacher. She had picked up a long item and was holding it with both hands, pointing to his feet. A stick? He stared at it in confusion.

"You have to trust me," she was saying, tears streaming down her face. "It's the only way. I don't want to hurt you, but we have to disconnect you…"

It wasn't a stick. It was a weapon, like a sword or a machete. A wide bladed curved thing, smooth with a sharp edge. Why did she have that?

"The Order controls you through the mark," her voice was breaking as she spoke through her tears. "And we have to take it off... They've been lying to you. You're not who you think you are..."

"I have found out the truth," he replied, though his senses were on alert. She was holding a weapon, and he was barred in the room with her. "I used to think I rescued children."

"You're a guardian now and you've done a lot of good, but that's not what you were before," she cried out. "Don't you remember?"

"Then I thought I was part of the Severance. That I had stolen away the boy, taken him from his family." He watched her arms with the weapon carefully.

"THEY are the Severance!" she was trembling now, lifting the sword off the ground, about at her knees.

"Then I discovered that I was the boy they stole," he said. He lifted his eyes to her face. "Did you know that?" he asked.

She nodded vehemently, tears streaming down her face, holding the blade a little higher.

"Why have I come to this house? I thought there was something in Caden's house, but I was wrong." He watched her face.

She nodded, weeping again. "I know, we blew that one, and I can't believe we got another chance. I thought I'd lost you forever..."

"The Cascade led me here."

"Yes." She swung the blade up high. "Will you trust me?" she cried out shrilly.

CASCADE

The other woman dove out the window across the room.

"Why are you threatening me?" He held up a hand to ward off the blade if she struck him, but his armor didn't darken. There was a desperate longing inside of him, rumbling like a sub-audible alarm, that resisted the trigger for rage.

The teacher cringed and her eyes filled with panic as his arm went up. She must know of the blades in the plate.

Outside a commotion broke out as Sentinels began to arrive and gather around the house. In minutes they were at the bedroom door banging on it. The sound activated his defenses and his armor darkened in response. Kierkad extended his arm toward her and tapped her chest with his fist with enough force to knock her back a step, ignoring the blade. He knew she didn't have the strength to do more than crack the armor.

"Oh my God! Don't you know me?" Terror filled her voice and her eyes. Taking a step backwards, she kept the weapon upraised. "I can do this..." she muttered under her breath.

Know me…. Know me…no me… Kier hesitated. The subversive had said that.

"Who are you?" he demanded, his voice thickened by the anger rising inside. He took a step closer, pressing his fist against her again, and the levered blade in his arm-plate unfurled, flashing its jagged edge, swinging close to her left arm.

She scrambled backward, nearly dropping the weapon, crying out, "No! No! Stop!!" choking on her sobs, and gritting her teeth, she gripped the handle with both hands again and raised it up between them.

"You…have…to…remember…me…"   she shoved the words past her lips and pressed the weapon against the arm with the jagged blade. It was a poor block, and her lack of skill surprised him.

"The Severance took me…" Kier said, leaning into her blade so that it touched his chest, daring her to strike him. "Why do you care?" Her hands were shaking now. Its weight was becoming too much for her.

"You were just a kid…"

"Who was the subversive in Caden's house?" he cut in, poising the tip of his knife at her throat.

"Your father died," she growled, backing away again till she bumped into the bed, eyes flaming, "trying to save you!" And with a clumsy thrust, she slammed her weapon against his right arm, against the piece of plate that covered the emblem.

Crrrraaaacckkkk! The wood of the door began to creak under the blows of the Sentinels.

Memory flashed. The man who had backed into the room, cornered by the other Sentinels, whose face had distorted into a wicked mocking creature… It was a lie. As he rejected the farce, the real memory returned. The face of the man crystalized in his mind. He saw him falling, wilting on the floor whispering, "Don't you know me?"

Kkkrrriinnnggg! The blade rang as she hit his arm-plate again, barely scratching it.

Kier stared at her.

"Please!" she cried incongruously, "help me!!"

Crrrraaaacckkkk! The door splintered. A black-armored, bladed arm burst through it, puncturing, tearing, fishing for the barricade that resisted it.

The teacher screamed and dropped her weapon, tumbling onto her back, scrabbling crablike toward the window.

"A subversive agent has been identified," the Sentinel broadcast into the room.

"You know me!" she shrieked at him, sobbing, choking, gasping for air, one hand stretched out to him in appeal. But her tears dried up as she gaped in horror at Kierkad.

He had grown dark again, responding to the Sentinel's call. Spinning around, he burst into movement, all six blades splayed, and began smashing the furniture in the room. He knocked out the lights and slammed pieces of broken furniture up against the door, wedging the bar more firmly in place.

A brief silence fell as Sentinels outside the door paused and Kier grew still.

"Who are you?" Kier whispered across the darkened, dust-filled space. Behind him in the hall, the brothers set up a great pounding again, fighting to free him. He felt the tug of the Order, pulling him, beckoning, reminding him of the strength of the bonds he shared with the brothers, reminding him of the high loyalty required by the Noble Call.

The promise of a higher task, setting things straight, making the Harbor a better place, wooed him. But somewhere, deeper inside, a lonely cry begged him to run with the woman, to listen to her.

"Why should I flee?" Kier raised his arms, one poised over the other, left arm blades aimed at the right arm, pausing for the answer.

Thud! Crash! Creak! The door behind him began to give way.

"Elex," she called out raggedly in the gloom, "Don't you remember?"

The name opened a world of memory, voices, tastes, smells, sounds, places, happiness, all in a jumble.

"Mom?" he whispered.

Half of the wall gave way as the Sentinels pushed their way through, with a deafening, tearing crash as the pieces collapsed blocking passage with rubble over a meter high that they had to crawl over to get in. The darkness and thick cloud of dust made it impossible to see.

As the echoes diminished, they heard a metallic ringing sound, a sharp crack, and a soft gush. Then all was still.

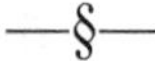

The satellite rotated patiently on one axis, then the second, and finally the third. Its new target had been identified, and it was locked on. The projectile was loaded into the gun, and a countdown started.

The count wasn't necessary. This was not a moving target and there was no trajectory to calculate to confirm the shot, but Mev wanted to wait for a few moments. He was still listening to the audio feed and heard the Sentinels reporting back on their progress. The old master was observed hungrily, every now and then commenting in his, Mevkad's, voice, giving a word of approval or an encouragement to have no mercy and crush the subversives.

"You may spare the brother," he said, "if he is willing to be taken. But don't let him escape."

He heard him laugh and mutter, "Any second now," as the Sentinels broke down the wall to the room where Kier was thought to be.

Yes, Mev agreed, and the gun belched its bomb, dropping it over the earth.

Seconds later it landed on the master's chambers at the Harbor and all communication ceased.

An invisible silvery thread stretching from the surface to the old satellite flickered out and the machine's gears never turned again. Set adrift, it watched over the valley until its batteries and solar panels flickered out, failing at last.

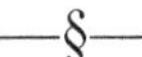

The way through the mazelike network of tunnels was twisted and hazardous. Kier—Elex—walked for hours in near total darkness, racked with pain from the gash on his forearm. It was self-inflicted. He had done what his mother lacked the strength to do and cut the link to the Harbor. Bandaged and strapped against his chest, it left him one arm to brace himself against the walls and keep from stumbling. Sometimes he leaned on his mother, sometimes on one of the others who had been there, waiting in the caverns below the town to help with his extraction.

No one spoke except to utter simple directions. The fear of capture hung over them, so did the threat of getting lost or being swept away by an underground stream bursting into a swell with a sudden rain.

The sound of tapping trailed down toward them, echoing through the uneven corridors before they could see any light.

"Message coming through," the scout leading the way said, turning over his shoulder.

His mother nodded and they sped up, traversing the last of the dark tunnel and breaking out into a vast, sparkling chamber, where a path wove down the side wall to a large human encampment. The sudden increase in light was blinding at first, but their eyes soon adjusted.

The underground cavern, where ancient waters once sculpted majestic crystal beauties, was lit by myriad lights strung in ropes across it. The clicking sound—a telegraph, archaic but by no means obsolete—was tapping out the latest report, speaking in an old code with updates for the human inhabitants who were stationed there.

People all around the camp paused in what they were doing, waiting for the operator to give the update.

"Ambrick Training Camp has been breached and twenty-six children rescued," a voice called out the news over an analog loudspeaker. "Four agents lost, presumed dead."

The tapping sounds continued.

"People," the voice went on, "Some of our own are in that number, two daughters and three sons…"

A hearty cheer burst out across the encampment, rich with clapping and hooting.

Elex felt the joy of the crowd, and sorrow mixed with it.

The announcement went on, "And one seasoned Sentinel from the Harbor Base."

Silence fell over the crowd. Lifting their faces toward the mouth of the tunnel, they saw the figures standing there, casting huge shadows behind them.

A wave of emotion rolled over them that swelled and broke into a roar of cheering and weeping that made the first cheer seem like a whimper.

Elex looked out over the people below, astonished. These men and women were welcoming him as if he were human, as if he belonged.

"How many have died saving Sentinels?" he whispered to his mother.

She seemed to understand his distress. "Son," she spoke softly, "when love compels you, the cost is never too high."

Kier thought of the subversive that he had helped put down, his father, who loved him more than the brothers and the Order ever could. The father who had died trying to save him. His eyes watered, and for the first time, a tear was allowed to escape.

A young man bolted out of the throng, barreling up the path to meet them, grabbing him in a fierce hug. "Brother!" Seda cried. "They wanted me to move on to the free world, but I would not. Not until I could see you were safe. I knew you would be coming soon. I knew it!"

Elex smiled. His face was pale and his eyes bloodshot, and he was so weak he couldn't walk without assistance, but his heart was full. There was no under-layer anymore. Just himself. The Harbor was gone. The emblem was gone.

As he shuffled his way down the path into the camp, a flurry of activity broke out. Reports were coming in of the destruction of the central command at the Harbor. Residents of the town were flooding the lines with calls for help and updates on the chaos breaking loose among the Sentinels. They were gearing up for response, throwing on packs, jogging up the path, barking orders, preparing for battle, injuries, and more rescues.

"I told them," Seda gripped Elex's shoulder, shaking it gently. "I said you would respond. You were detaching from the Harbor. I could see it."

"I..." Elex said, his voice cracking dryly, "I almost didn't. The Brothers, there are so many now...

If I had stayed, I could have helped them. But I didn't know if...about the danger..."

"All this?" Seda waved his arm in a wide arc around the cavern at the flurry of activity among the tents. "Everyone here, joined for that very purpose, and right now, they are running to rescue more of our brothers. And with the Harbor's destruction, they will be easier to reason with because their home is gone."

"Why?" Elex's eyes were hollow with weariness, and the idea penetrated his understanding with difficulty. "We have oppressed them. *We* are the Severance. Don't they know that?"

Seda's gaze flashed with pain with the memory of things he had done, but he swallowed and nodded. "They know," he answered soberly, "and many of them…many have died to rescue us one by one."

Elex hung his head and thought of his father. Despite having no clear memory of him, it ached like a gaping wound in his chest. "I don't understand." He hadn't realized yet, though the teacher had called herself his mother, and he had the idea of a father—that he was human.

"They are saving their children," Seda whispered. "That's who we are. We weren't the Severance; we were just their hostages."

"And they still wanted us after…what we became?"

Seda nodded, his eyes glistening with emotion. "There is no hatred or rage in their love for us. And they have paid whatever cost was necessary to get us back."

"The camps are falling," Elex volunteered, remembering the map in the Pacificator's room.

"Yes," Seda said with thin smile. "And now that the Harbor AI is destroyed, they have nothing left."

Elex echoed the smile with a wan one of his own and closed his eyes. A surge of hope that was almost more than he could contain caused his heart to pound.

Not a Sentinel any longer. This planet was his own.

He was home.

The invasion of Earth had wiped out every governing structure on the planet, establishing an order that brought peace at a terrible cost. But when all was lost, hope nearly quenched, and the crushing grip of the Severance hardening into permanence around them, a remnant found a way to resist. A few escaped among the stars and some hid underground.

They snatched hope from the jaws of despair and, against all odds, turned the tide. Because they knew that even at the darkest hour of an eclipse, the sun glows with a ring of light.

And once it passes, the shadow is gone.

The End

CASCADE

ECLIPSE

Who was behind the Cascade?

A thriving scientific community lived in orbit around the Earth, tending the Reticulary, a solar power harvesting structure. When the Jagged Edge took over the planet, they wiped them out, trusting in AI to manage the system.

They missed a few.

The rebels on the surface were failing until they discovered allies in space and the tide began to turn. If they knew they were there —the Order of Peace would have no trouble crushing Pitch and her fellow Specs.

Now the underground can't survive without them, the enemy doesn't understand their tactics, and supplies in space are running out.

Then Pitch discovers the terrible truth about the Sentinels...and why they must fight to the bitter end.

Eclipse, the sequel to Cascade covers about two and half years and the events in Cascade happen over a three week period near the end of that time. The sequel is a must-read to understand the full picture of what has happened.

About the Author

Suzanne Hagelin is a USA Today bestselling author who writes mostly science fiction with plausible science set in the near future. She has lived as varied and interesting a life as she could manage—growing up in Mexico City, living in the Middle East, traveling and exploring the world, learning languages, working in IT, family, exchange students, teaching, volunteering, and translating. She settled in the Seattle area where she runs an indie publishing company, Varida P&R, with a small group of authors, and teaches language on the side.

Find out more at Suzannehagelin.com.

Books by this author:

Available in print, digital, and audiobook formats.

The Silvarian Trilogy:

> Book 1— "BODY SUIT" A clever woman in a high-tech suit versus a hostile AI…on Mars.

> Book 2— "NEBULUS" Human warfare is changing, and the AIs are taking sides.

> Book 3— "THE DENSER PLANE" Opposing planes are skewed by human, AI, and alien forces.

The Severance includes two books:

> Book 1— "CASCADE" A space virus threatens the guardians of the earth.

> Book 2— "ECLIPSE" Besides taking down the Sentinel camps, the Specs have plans for the earth.